"Jesus, you have visitors. Mary coaxed the child out from his shyness. He giggled. The kind of gleeful belly-laugh only a toddler can share. She leaned down, playing with his curly chestnut hair. Jesus grasped two fingers of her graceful hand as she guided him out from behind her skirts.

Jesus had his mother's nose and mouth, but his eyes… Nike had never seen such eyes.

"He has his Father's eyes," Mary explained.

The clock is ticking as the Roman Empire faces the great imperium Parthia in an unexpected confrontation.

Parthia has sent their Wisemen, the Magi, to find the King of Kings and the wary Romans and murderous tetrarch, Herod, are watching closely.

And at the nexus of these two great superpowers is a child who will change the world.

MAGI'S
CHRISTMAS...
33 Years to Easter

NOEL THORNLEY

Printed in the United States
ISBN-10: 1517513898
ISBN-13: 978-1517513894

Art work: Panos Lampridis
Edited by Kristina Kugler

Praise For
Magi's Christmas

By Don Kidwell Amazon TOP 1000 REVIEWER

A curious blend of two tales including the birth of Christ and the coming of Santa Claus. An offbeat Christmas story where those items most associated with Jesus' death. . .are transferred into the symbols we associate with Santa. For a different type of read, this one certainly stands out!

By workerbevon

OUTSTANDING!
I was sad when the story ended. How the author tied Jesus birth to the Magi's quest to St Nickolas is outstanding! The miracles, day to day life, and love, no words can describe it better. I will forever remember this story, so poignant.

By Tresta Neilon

This a very clever fiction book about the life of a "magi" and his friend as they follow the life of Christ. The ending will leave you thinking. The ideas in this book have changed the way I look at Christmas.

By Cheri Jacobson

Before you get lost in the hustle and bustle (or if you unfortunately already have) do yourself and your loved ones a favor and pick up this book. It is a treasure that you can share with Family and Friends for years to come.

By David Willden

What a riveting book! The author provides incredible insights into the Christmas Story in a way that captures your emotions and your complete attention. You can image the surroundings, you see characters in rich detail, and most importantly you feel the intense emotions, The Christmas story will never be the same. You will develop a whole new love and appreciation for what really happened.

See and feel the emotions for what really happened in a way that completely captures your emotions and attention.

By Stephanie Allen Egbert

I particularly appreciated the scene where the Magi are introduced to Mary, Joseph, and the Christ child because you help me visualize just how beautiful in spirit and purity they were and how they may have appeared. I also loved the part where Nike is preparing his report to the Magi Council. . .where he explains Jesus' divinity. Oh, how beautiful those words were!

Thank you for the spiritual feast and for helping me envision the Savior with greater clarity. I was moved spiritually and emotionally.

DEDICATION

For dad who lives Christmas, and celebrates Easter, every day.

Chapter 1

TO BE FREE

They sat in a silent circle, every eye on the ancient tribal leader. The chief sat cross legged with his hands resting in his lap. Next to him was an American officer, sitting in the same manner, distracted by the patterns in the Persian carpet covering parts of the hard packed dirt floor. Some coolness emanated from the earth this warm autumn morning.

The chief's leather face, folded by a million smiles and thousands of new suns, waited patiently, adjusting the keffiyeh worn on his head in the Kurdish fashion. Everyone in the room, except the American officer, wore one, giving the impression of a circle of solemn mushrooms.

"Captain Bixby."

The chief's curious voice interrupted a thought the captain had been nursing from early that morning. He hadn't seen his family in eight months. He pushed the thought aside to focus on why he was there, on why he had sacrificed those eight months. The chief leaned over and looked up into the captain's pensive face, smiling a tea-stained grin to get his attention. "Captain, Sir!"

"There are others, not my people, afraid of this agreement but my tribe wants this peace. Many of us believe in the ways of Jesus. They believe you bring the greatest possibility of this freedom." The solemn mushrooms in the circle broke cautious smiles, looking at each other, and nodding in agreement.

"You and your people have risked so much to bring freedom to this region. Why?"

In reply, the old man smiled shyly, and reached into his coat to produce a timeworn, leather text. He turned to face Captain Bixby and explained.

"This ancient story has been passed from our fathers around the dinner fire, and sung by our mothers as they rocked us to sleep. But over hundreds of years of peace and war, and attacks on our faith, it became an inaudible whisper and was nearly lost."

"Originally this story was shared in our oral tradition. But, our fathers and mothers, sensing the story's loss, wrote it down over many generations. This is why we seek to bring freedom here, because we love Jesus, and to love Jesus is to be free. Please, this is a gift from our people."

At that instant the abrupt pops of automatic weapons fire tore the air, startling the council, causing panic and confusion. Everyone in the room dove for cover but as the captain looked to the chief he saw no fear in his face, only concern for the text clutched against his chest.

The screams of children and the shouts of soldiers and villagers came from all directions. Captain Bixby sprang towards the old Chief to protect him, but the blast was faster, smashing the Captain face first into the dirt. Brick fragments, and a thick, fine cloud of dust erupted, coating everyone and everything.

Captain Bixby pushed himself up from the floor onto his hands and knees. Shaking his head, his ears ringing, he closed his eyes tight against the dust that coated his face.

"Who's hurt?" He choked out, spitting blood and mud from his mouth. Then, blinking to clear his sight, he scanned the room, quickly assessing the situation. Part of the back wall of the house was obliterated by a rocket propelled grenade that impacted nearby.

To his relief, everyone seemed to be more shaken than hurt, moving like shadows in a gray-brown fog, coughing and staggering towards a way out.

Then, as he scanned the room for the Chief, he saw his old friend's still form partially covered by rubble and timber. The only color in the monochrome, dust-filled, room was a terrible red gash to the side of the chief's head.

"Medic! MEDIC!" Captain Bixby yelled as he removed the debris that covered his friend. He was sure the Chief was dead, but out of the brick and debris a desperate hand reached up and grasped the front of his tactical vest, pulling him down to the old man's face. Then his voice rasped into the Captain's ear.

"Keep the story safe . . . never lose it. I go to a good place with Jesus." He let out a ragged, final breath and his hand fell to his chest. Captain Bixby tried to revive his friend and stop the bleeding as a medic rushed through the confusion to help. The medic yelled into the old man's face, asking him questions, but he couldn't respond. He was gone.

Close behind the medic Sergeant Bixby climbed through the rubble, coughing and futilely waving his hand as if it could clear the dust so he could see better. His first concern, the safety of his captain, caused him to call out, almost panicking, even as he spotted the commander with a medic bent over someone on the floor.

Two silver strings, like tiny streams, trailed down the commander's dust-caked face, dripping off his chin into muddy spatters on the ground. He bowed his head allowing that ache in his heart to return that accompanied the loss of a brother or sister in arms. The pain caused him to remember others he had lost in defense of freedom. He welcomed the ache just as he welcomed joy and friendship, for to forget the pain would mean to forget the joy.

Captain Bixby regained his composure as he stood up, smearing the evidence of his sadness into muddy camouflage.

"Sergeant Bixby!" he said. "Did we lose anyone else?" Then in a quieter, pleading voice, "Any children?"

The Sergeant replied kindly, understanding Captain Bixby's passion for protecting children, "Only minor injuries, except our friend." The sergeant nodded towards the fallen chief. "No children were hurt," There was a brief moment of certain silence, then the Sergeant spoke again. "Are you going to be okay Bro?" The Captain responded with a barely perceptible, weary nod.

Sergeant Bixby noticed an old leather book on the ground nearby. He bent down to pick it up, shaking dust from between its ancient pages.

"This important?" he queried as he discreetly squeezed his brother's arm and handed him the ancient leather tome.

"It was to him," Captain Bixby whispered bending down to cover the tribal leader's face with the shemagh scarf he had around his neck. "I'll start translating it and tell you when I understand what it's about."

The town's people and leaders had crowded outside the door to gather the old chief's body for burial. Captain Bixby expressed his sadness for the loss of a great man and explained that he and his team would remain in the area until a new leader was chosen and negotiations could begin again.

Sergeant Bixby was a taller, broader version of the Captain. The brothers could have been twins, except the Captain had unruly black hair and the Sergeant's hair and beard were copper, making him look in need of a kilt and broad sword.

Captain Bixby's mouth was still bleeding as the town's people took their beloved leader's body away. The Sergeant handed him a gauze pad soaked with disinfectant. "Captain, your mouth is still bleeding badly. You might have the medic take a look at that." The Captain winced, and his eyes watered as he applied the gauze to stop the bleeding. Sergeant Bixby then hesitated as he considered the best way, as he had promised before the negotiations, to remind his older brother about his daughter's birthday. He decided to be direct.

"Oh, by the way, did you remember Agnes' birthday is today?"

"Yeth," Captain Bixby replied through the bandage. The medic handed him some more gauze and started examining the Captain's injured mouth. "I woke up early this morning..."

"Ouch! Go easy man!" Captain Bixby growled.

"Sorry," The medic apologized with an embarrassed smile.

He started to explain again after the medic had finished temporary treatment of the wound. "I woke up early this morning thinking about it, and it's been in the back of my mind since then. This is the second time I've missed her birthday."

Sergeant Bixby nodded distractedly as he remembered, gratefully, that his brother's family had become his family also since their parent's passing and a string of unsuccessful relationships back in the States.

"You're a lucky man Newt. You've got a great wife and kids." The Captain smiled and shook his head wearily. "I really don't deserve them. They have given up so much. Sometimes I wonder who sacrifices more, the soldier's families or the warriors themselves."

Chapter 2

WAITING FOR SANTA

Agnes had just turned fifteen and Newt had about worn out being eleven. They could have been twins if it weren't for the fact Newt shared his dad's unruly black hair and dark eyes. Agnes' hair was a copper mop, like her uncle's, and her eyes were brilliant green. Besides those minor differences, they could have been twins.

What Agnes lacked in faith she made up with love, and she loved her little brother and hated it if he were disappointed. She struggled to control her frustration when people teased Newt, even good naturedly, or laughed behind his back. At eleven, he still believed in Santa, and loved to sing or whistle Christmas carols through the whole year. Perhaps she was jealous of his simple faith. Even as their world crumbled around them Newt chose to be happy.

Newt was a true believer, and a genuine optimist. His dark eyes were made more intense by his kind and open face. When he smiled, which he did frequently, it was difficult for anyone near him to be unhappy. Newt Jr. was a small version of Newt Sr., who had the same happy problem as his son. They were relentless optimists. When a door closed in their face, it just meant a new door was opening somewhere else.

But it was Agnes who started the tradition of sitting at the front door Christmas Eve to wait for her father and for Santa. It started when she was only three. She taught this to Newt as a child and he believed every word and story from Agnes about Christmas. When her father went Missing in Action just before Christmas the stories stopped for Agnes.

"Newt, why do you wait by the front door for Dad every Christmas Eve?" She asked.

Newt turned from the door, his dark eyes smiling. "Why do you ask me the same question every Christmas Eve?"

Agnes resisted saying something skeptical. She was fighting her little brother's hope that rattled the door knob of her heart.

Agnes decided to be direct, "After three years Missing in Action what makes you believe Dad is coming home?"

Turning back to face the door, he responded. "That's why they call it *missing* in action, not *killed* in action. This could be the Christmas he comes back. If anyone can do it Dad can!"

Newt's confidence started an ember in Agnes' core. The warmth increased and rose up through her chest, into her face, and spilled out her eyes as healing tears. Just for a moment, a wonderful moment, Agnes knew Dad was finally coming home. She imagined him walking up to the house with Mom, who was holding onto his strong arm, her black hair pressed against his shoulder with that wisp of gray hair blowing across her eyes. But then the reality of their father's death, that Newt continued to ignore, welled up and chilled the illusion of Dad ever coming home, and made those tears cold on her cheeks. The pain of Dad being gone pushed back hard. And now she was mad.

Agnes hadn't been this angry since she'd heard Dad was missing. Accusations, doubt, jealousy; a cyclone of emotions, almost blinded her to the innocence and faith of her brother. She could have screamed at Newt she was so furious. She wanted to shout, "Dad is dead! Neither he nor Santa is coming through that stupid door. Accept it!"

But love curbed the anger, and instead of yelling at Newt, Agnes jumped up and stumbled to the front door, throwing it open, and charged into the night. Escaping into the darkness she plowed into her uncle's broad chest, causing her mother to let go of Uncle Bix's arm to catch her. She brushed a gray wisp of hair away from her eyes as she looked into Agnes's anguished face.

"What's wrong, baby?" she said, wrapping her arms around her trembling shoulders pressing her cheek to her sobbing daughter's. Agnes could feel the tears on her mother's face, and when she looked up at Uncle Bix, she could see he'd been crying too.

In that instance, the fragile spark of hope left behind in the house, was extinguished. Agnes didn't know how, but she knew, she knew Dad wasn't coming home. Agnes's world began spinning as Uncle Bix and Mom helped her back into the house.

Chapter 3

First Christmas Eve...

Newt was still recovering from the confusion of Agnes's abrupt exit when Mom and Uncle Bix half carried her back into the house and helped her to the couch.

"Is she OK?" exclaimed Newt, moving to help. Just as the words left his mouth he looked into their faces, and he knew what they knew.

Agnes couldn't look at Newt. She'd just seen the death of her own feeble hopes. Newt's broken heart would be too much. She could only handle one loss that night.

"Newt . . . Newt, look at me," his mother said quietly. Newt stood anchored to the floor. He stared down in a numb stupor.

"Dad couldn't be gone," he prayed. "Dad couldn't die. He's always returned from every mission." Newt's prayers had always been answered. His faith had always been rewarded.

"Newt!" He heard his mom's voice echo from down a long tunnel. He started shuffling towards her until her strong arms hugged him to her chest and they sat down on the couch.

Agnes sat on one side of her mother, sobbing quietly, with little stuttering hiccups, her eyes puffy and red from crying, glancing over at Uncle Bix furtively, as if all this was his fault. She knew it wasn't, but just couldn't help the feelings of resentment. Uncle Bix had been the last one to see their dad. Newt just sat there, with his head against his mother's shoulder, staring at his hands in his lap as if they were somebody else's, feeling a crowbar at his heart, and the first challenge to his faith he could remember.

Bix seemed lost as his six-two frame wandered towards the front door, placing his hand on its surface and bowing his head.

At that moment of sorrow, Mom drew her children closer, and gently called to her grieving brother-in-law.

"Bix, since Newt went missing we've kept Christmas Eve to ourselves. Just the three of us. Please share it with us tonight."

Uncle Bix found his way to a worn, red leather chair that was traditionally Agnes' nest. He leaned his face into his hands across from the sofa where Erin and her children sat. The simple act of Bix sitting in Agnes' personal perch caused her to look up and the sobbing to cease. People rarely sat in Agnes's red chair. It was the chair that her father had snuggled her in, and read stories to her when she was little. It was her place, and Uncle Bix had just sat in it.

Bix took a deep breath, lifted his face from his hands and asked, "How do you suggest we celebrate Christmas Eve?"

"Tell us about the last time you saw Dad," Agnes asked in a subdued voice. "We've never heard what happened."

Bix looked toward the front door, considering the possibility of escape. Then he turned to face the only family he had left.

"I've been using the excuse that the incident was classified to avoid telling you . . . I didn't know how to tell you." Bix's face and shoulders strained. His large, powerful hands opened and closed as he struggled with how to explain. Then he just said it.

"It's my fault your Dad was lost. I left him when he needed me to have his back. I left him alone."

The confused and stunned looks on Agnes and Newt's faces confirmed his deepest fears, and even Bix was amazed he'd said the words. He looked down and put his face in his hands. He'd lost his brother and his Captain, and now was about to lose the only family he had left.

"Look at me, Bix," said Erin. His head didn't budge. "Bix. Look at me."

Slowly Special Forces Sergeant Bixby did the hardest thing he'd ever done. He looked up.

Erin looked back into his face. There was subtle terror veiling Bix's eyes.

"Bix, we've always trusted you." Bix's large frame shrank back in the chair as he locked eyes with his sister-in-law's fervent gaze. "Both you and I know you'd have never abandoned Newt. You'd die first."

Bix had been trying to outrun his regret and guilt ever since his brother went MIA. Technically he knew it wasn't his fault but felt he could have done something different. Something more. Something that would have brought his brother home to his family. He didn't visit Erin and the kids as much anymore, and frequently found excuses to be out of town, or he would volunteer for extra duty. He should have been the one lost, not Newt. Bix was so busy running from the pain, he evaded the healing influence of those who loved him most.

He had been expecting anger or rejection. This faithful vote of confidence caused a kind of joyous shock. His sister-in-law was a beautiful woman, but right now she made the angels look plain.

"Tell us the truth, Bix. Tell us what you can. We have your back."

Bix, for the first time in a long time, felt safe. His voice was quiet.

"The last time I saw Newt," he looked at the children, "your father, he was moving into the dark towards the enemy. With night vision, and a heavy machine gun, he was able to suppress the enemy long enough to evacuate the wounded. If it hadn't been for Newt, we'd have been evacuating the dead."

"We were pinned down in a small canyon at the foot of a steep, rocky mountain. We were pursuing a group of Iranian-backed insurgents who'd been disrupting our attempts to bring peace to the region. Newt sensed an ambush, so he called in air support and started moving us away from danger. But we were attacked by the enemy before support arrived. The heavy enemy fire made it impossible to evacuate the last of the wounded. At that point, he made a crucial choice. One man would stay behind to provide cover fire and space for the injured. That's where he gave me a direct order to get the wounded to the evacuation chopper, then to come back for him. I resisted. But my argument was cut short by his command."

"As he reached down and picked up the heavy machine gun, he turned and yelled over the confusion of combat. "I'll hold them until you get the wounded on the chopper and come back with reinforcements. Air support is coming. Then, to encourage Bix he called out with a laugh, 'We'll read that Story the Chief gave us Christmas Eve together with my family!' That's the last time I saw your dad."

Everyone was quiet. No one spoke, all lost in their own thoughts and remembering the man they loved. They wouldn't see him again in this life. After a long moment, that no one measured, Agnes spoke.

"Did you find the story and translation?" Agnes leaned forward expectantly. "What was so special about the book?"

Uncle Bix took a deep breath and sighed. "Your dad told me it was something significant about Christmas. That's all I know. I couldn't find the translation, and the story is missing."

Erin didn't say anything, but her face showed everyone's frustration.

"Can't this family catch a break?" Agnes lamented.

Agnes slumped back into the couch cushions while Uncle Bix looked down and ran his hands through his tight-cropped red hair.

By this time, Newt had stood up and looked at the front door, then back to where his bedroom was.

"We don't need the original text to read the story," he yelled back over his shoulder as he ran to his bedroom.

He returned with a large folder of papers. "I had the story in my room!" He exclaimed, as he returned, somewhat breathless. "Dad translated the meaning of the original text than wrote a story based on the translation to share with the family when he returned. He sent the story to me in his letters, making me promise I'd keep it a secret so we could read it as a family Christmas Eve. I've been waiting for Dad to come home so we could read it together. I know he'd want us to read it tonight."

Pleasant astonishment and curiosity temporarily softened the pain. The atmosphere changed from hopelessness to anticipation. Newt, with his broad grin, flipped through the hand written, dog eared sheets, as he had countless times anticipating the joy of reading the Christmas Story his father had written and sent to him for safe keeping until he returned.

He held the story out to Bix, Newt's whole body vibrating. "Uncle Bix, please read the story to us," Newt pleaded with his uncle, then looked towards his mother, hoping she'd convince him to stay and read the story with them.

"What type of a Christmas story is it?" Bix asked reaching for the well loved and worn pages. Pages that were a Christmas promise kept by a young boy who now longed to enjoy the reward of his faith.

"It's a story about the Wise Men's visit to the child Jesus," Newt announced with a small shudder of excitement. "I started to read it, but then decided to wait for Dad to come back."

Just holding the story his brother wrote triggered that regret again and he looked for an excuse for someone else to read. "You know I don't believe in religious stuff Newt." Uncle Bix started to hand the letters back, but he looked up into Newt's eyes — his brother's eyes — and he saw the same faith he'd seen the night he lost his Captain and his best friend. Bix had to read the story.

Chapter Four

JERUSALEM

"You fool, open your eyes! You know the penalty for sleeping on watch if you're caught!" A small pebble flew from the same direction as the warning bouncing harmlessly off the drowsy soldier's helmet. The dozing Roman sentry stirred and grumbled, but still leaned heavily on his spear. Then, for some inexplicable reason, his eyes flew open and he looked up. Squinting into the morning's horizon, he sensed something, then he felt a vibration — a movement in the air — and then he heard it: the distant thunder of ten thousand flint hooves. Billowing dust clouds swelled into the crimson morning, the sun flashing off seemingly endless banners, lances, and armor.

"Look . . . look! Can you see them? Can you see them?" The newly awake sentry yelled, pointing out toward the approaching mass of horse and rider. The other guards on the wall stared, frozen in disbelief. It was Parthian cavalry. Cold fear rose into their hearts. The stories of

Parthian cavalry from beyond the Euphrates, like the hoard rolling toward Jerusalem now, were told over watch fires and in mess halls. Legends of the Parthian wars, where dozens of Roman legions were decimated in savage conflict were still remembered. Tales of the sheer brutality of huge, steel clad war horses, and clouds of devastating arrows caused the sentries to pause in disbelief before reality reached their voices.

The Sentries screamed from the walls, "Assemble the cohorts! Assemble the cohorts!" In moments, hundreds of yelling men were spilling out of their barracks, stumbling and swearing, fumbling with their shields while strapping on their armor and weapons.

The once sleepy soldier looked back at the fast approaching horde and despair turned to amazement. The cavalry's banners announced something extraordinary. They spoke not of war, but of the coming of the Magi: Makers of Kings.

Chapter Five

THE KING'S MEN

The Roman legionaries stared forward, standing at attention in rigid lines, row upon row, in respect for the Magi dignitaries. The air was thick with dust and the sour odor of men and horses ridden on a hot morning. From time to time, a soldier would sneeze — drawing a displeased glance from the Legate Commander. Cradling his helmet under one arm, he greeted the Wise Men with a stiff bow. His attention was immediately drawn to the imposing Magi at the center of the delegation.

All eyes were now on this towering Magi Chief. He was splendid, and he knew it. His chiseled face and magnificent nose were amplified by the fire in his eyes. His brilliant orange robes and armor dazzled as he took the Roman commander's hand ceremoniously in his large and powerful grasp. "I am Nike, Prime Magistrate." He drawled.

The Commander and his Praefectus exchanged nervous glances. This remarkable Parthian magistrate was no one to be trifled with. Nike smiled. He could see a fleck of fear in the Legate's eyes. He had that effect.

"If it please you, my lords, one of my aides will help your men find a suitable place for water and rest outside the city while we escort you to your objective. You have traveled a great distance. What has brought you so far beyond the Euphrates?"

Nike paused, and then turned to the other Wise Men. Their eyes met and they all nodded in agreement. Nike turned back to the Roman Commander.

"Where is he that is born King of the Jews? For we have seen his star in the East and are come to worship him."

The answer to his question somewhat startled the unflapable Roman and the Commander turned to his assistant, "I will personally escort our visitors to their destination. Provide two detachments to accompany us from the First Cohort."

Chapter Six

No Other Kings

Herod heard of the Wise Men's search for the New King. He was troubled — and all Jerusalem with him. He called the scribes and priests to audience.

"You claim to know the law . . . You claim to know the people . . . You claim to know God's will!" Herod's voice hissed with venom as he pointed out a large window. "Now Parthian Magi from the distant East arrive seeking one who is born King of the Jews!" How do they know of this child and you do not? The priests and scribes could only look down at the fringed hems of their robes. They didn't dare look up into Herod's petulant face.

Herod, impatient with no answers, and their incoherent muttering to each other, went from cold and deadly to distraught and fierce screaming until his voice cracked, spraying spittle across his chamber. "I am the King of the Jews! I AM THE KING! THERE ARE NO OTHER KINGS!"

And then, just as abruptly he transformed into a different person. Herod leaned back and returned to his cold, deadly voice. "Where do the scriptures say this king will be born?"

The scribes and priests hesitated. Even their soiled souls recoiled at Herod's motives. They were quite aware of his murderous history, but the desire for self preservation overcame their consciences.

"Where?" Herod prodded sweetly with a smile.

The priests cleared their vulnerable throats, still looking at their feet, one mumbled, "In Bethlehem of Judaea: For thus it is written by the prophet. . . "

Herod stared at the priest, who had answered his question, with an amused smirk on his face, gloating, "Now that wasn't so hard was it?" Then looking away, he flippantly motioned with a wave of his hand toward the priests and scribes, as if to sweep them from his presence. "Go make yourselves useful against the wall," he jeered.

The flock of scribes shuffled to the place Herod had swept them, murmuring their disapproval, where they suffered in silence against the wall.

Herod motioned to his steward, and whispering urgent instructions, then quickly sent him off with an escort to invite the Magi to audience.

Chapter Seven

THE KING MAKERS

More than a dozen Magi and their attendants entered Herod's great hall. Some wore ornate armor, others fine embroidered tunics and trousers. The armor and the Magi sparkled, framed by rich cloaks, robes of deep reds, blazing yellows, and saturated blues. Even Herod was astonished as he stood and welcomed the Wise Men, trying to expand himself, pretending to be unimpressed.

"Welcome! Welcome, my lords. Peace be unto you. I hope you've found your visit pleasant. How do you find my beautiful city?" Herod raised his hands as if to present some great wonder. "Are the buildings as fine as those in Greece, or Rome . . . or Persia?" Herod asked, hoping for some adulation from someone other than the boring locals — someone who knew beauty and greatness.

"We find your city lovely and equal to any we've seen," Melchior lied with a forced smile. They had been warned by the Roman's, and Jewish nobility alike, that Herod could be unpredictable.

Herod smiled at the flattery and leaned back against his cushioned throne, as he seated himself again, content with the compliment.

"So," he started, "We've been told of this star and a king you have come to worship. When did you first see this prophetic sign?" He inquired nonchalantly, inspecting his greasy fingertips.

Nike parried the direct question with a question of his own. "Do you also desire to worship the young king?"

Herod had no intention of worshiping anyone. He was a political animal and found satisfaction only in worshiping himself. But now he knew the "king" was in Bethlehem and he was a child. All he needed to know now was the time the star was first seen.

"Yes, you read my mind my friend," Herod laughed I also desire to visit the young king. My council believes the young prince may be in Bethlehem. Perhaps you will find him there?"

Moved by the enthusiasm of the moment Gaspar exclaimed. "The star has brought us this far and beckons us in Bethlehem's way. Since the great sign appeared nearly two years ago we assembled the bravest and wisest Magi in Parthia to worship the king announced by the heavenly sign. Why shouldn't Herod also join us in our quest" As the words left his mouth, Nike and the other Magi knew a grave mistake had just been made.

Though no changes came to Herod's face, something malignant veiled his eyes. Then he spoke.

"How do lions of Parthia find themselves in my small corner of the world? The Magi choose kings for Parthia. Why are you here?" Then he raised himself up and looked into the Wise Men's faces, his voice becoming ominous.

"We already have a king here."

The Magi felt something indescribable from Herod that caused them to fear for the Child of the Star. Then, as if a sweet, fragrant spring breeze stirred through Herod, he leaned back with a pleasant smile. The sudden personality change rattled the Magi's legendary composure and they knew they would be wise men to go quickly.

Nike looked narrowly at Herod and cleared his throat. "We thank you for your attentiveness to our errand , but we must take our leave." The Magi bowed, backing away, Nike never taking his eyes off Herod.

As the Magi moved toward the safety of their Roman escort, Herod raised his hand toward them.

"My lords, not so fast, I've a request." Herod smiled a threatening grimace, and everyone in the room shivered in spite of the warmth of the late afternoon. "Go and search diligently for the young child. Bring me word when you find the new king so that," he hesitated, "so that I might worship him also."

Somehow, the words did not sound like a request.

"We have endangered the very king we came to supplicate!" Nike muttered audibly as the Magi rushed past their Roman escort. "We must make haste to Bethlehem tonight!" Nike voice was not pleased as he rushed ahead.

Of all the wonders seen in the world, no one had ever seen a quorum of Magi running.

Chapter Eight

Six Miles to Bethlehem

"Look! Look! The star. See how it guides us," cried Nike, as they mounted fresh horses outside the city walls. From the back of his eager mount he instructed the Parthian Commander to follow with the full cavalry, and support caravan, and make camp outside Bethlehem. The Magi would go ahead and meet them back at camp.

Nike wheeled his horse towards Bethlehem and he and the other Wise Men rode hard following the star that led them to where the smell of bread and evening meals still hung in the air.

The light of the star guided the Wise Men to a well kept little home and workshop. They dismounted and stood outside with their precious gifts for the king.

"This is not what I'd expected of a prince announced by the very heavens," wondered Balthazar.

Nike, who had been mostly silent since the unfortunate meeting with Herod, replied earnestly. "The prophecies and the star have brought us to this unusual place. This is not what we had expected, but consider, my brothers. To this point, we have chosen rulers from the ranks of the famous and powerful. What has it brought the empire? Uneasy peace between Rome and Parthia. Intrigue. Disunity. War. Perhaps this is the king who will unify the nations. Who is this child the very heavens declare, despots fear, and we find in this humble place?"

Just then, a solitary man stepped out from the shadow of a doorway and spoke. "I am Joseph. Why have you come from so far away to our humble home?" Joseph looked up into the night sky. Then, with his eyes still on the star, he wondered out loud, "It's been many months since the star first appeared. Why do men of your rank come to a little village on the border of two great empires? Whom do you seek?"

Nike stepped forward, impressed with the nobility of this man unadorned by the trappings of power and wealth. Bowing slightly and looking into Joseph's face, he spoke. "We are Magi from the East, come to worship the king of the Jews — your son."

Joseph bowed his face with the palms of his hands gently raised in protest. "I am of the line of David, but the

child you seek is not my son. His Father . . . his Father is .
. . " Joseph's voice trailed off.

The Magi noted the genuine wonder and reverence
with which he spoke. They hesitated to enter the presence
of this great prince who needed neither palace, nor armies,
nor the devices of power to guard him.

Nike spoke again — more humbly this time. Embers
he had never felt before kindled in his heart. "We implore
that we be given a brief audience to bestow a portion of
our modest gifts. We have come so far."

Joseph held open the door of his home and ushered
the Magi in.

Chapter Nine

Epiphany

The Magi entered the humble home with ardent anticipation, not sure what to expect from already unusual royal circumstances. What first they saw was even more extraordinary than the light they had already seen.

The young mother who stood before them embodied a singularity of virtue that caused them to hesitate, unsure how to approach. Nike had counseled with the world's most powerful and beautiful. He had never encountered anyone like this.

"My lords, peace be unto you. Welcome to our home," Mary greeted the Wise Men. Nike, though tall and powerful, felt like a child in the presence of this wonderful mother. He hesitated.

"We are honored at your presence," came Mary's kind words.

The Magi seemed unsure how to proceed, enchanted by Mary's grace and remarkable beauty. No face paint, no silks, no jewelry. Nike had heard the legends of Esther, but only now could realize what they meant.

"Please, be at ease," Mary encouraged the Magi to come forward to meet her son.

The child was playing a game behind Mary with the folds of her robe, peaking out from behind his mother, then hiding again, then flashing a bright smile, then hiding his face again. Brief glimpses of piercing eyes and an open face appeared, and then disappeared, as he swept the hem of his mother's robe back and forth.

"Jesus, you have visitors." Mary coaxed the child out from his shyness. He giggled. The kind of gleeful belly-laugh, and gift, only a toddler can share. She leaned down, playing with his curly chestnut hair. Jesus grasped two fingers of her graceful hand as she guided him out from behind her skirts.

Jesus had his mother's nose and mouth, but his eyes… Nike had never seen such eyes.

"He has his Father's eyes," Mary explained, smiling as Nike stared in amazement into the child's face. Embers, like the coals in the child's eyes, burned into the Magi's hearts with a joy they had never before known. Something beyond their understanding compelled them to fall to the earth. Nike only dared look up because he could not take his eyes off the wonderful child.

Jesus placed his dimpled hand on Nike's cheek and touched the tears streaming down his face, splashing on the hard dirt floor. He was loved. This child knew him and all his pride, fears, and weaknesses. And yet, he was still loved.

"What a *wonderful* child," Nike murmured, bowing his head and trying to remember everything about this divine moment as the child danced among the other Wise Men, greeting them one by one. Patting their faces, touching their foreheads, and rumpling their beards. His words were simple and kind as he touched a ring here, or an amulet there, and smiled. Jesus liked moving his hands through the folds of their robes, delighted by the different textures and colors.

The evening, lit only by oil lamps and a small cook fire, seemed to have limitless light and warmth. This small, humble home was more hallowed than any temple or palace. The Magi could not understand what they were feeling. Fervent sobs punctuated the evening as several grasped the front of their robes over their hearts and closed their eyes, trying to understand. Many of them could not speak.

The Magi only now remembered their gifts, but gold, frankincense, and myrrh seemed wholly inadequate to express their adoration. Jesus toddled over to the Magi holding the casket of myrrh, wrapping his little arms around it. The Magi looked up at Mary for direction.

"He's trying to bring it to me," Mary spoke with a pleased smile on her face. "He wants to help. Go ahead and let him try."

Jesus was amazed at the weight of the casket as he looked to his mother for help. He strained, trying not to drop the myrrh as he wobbled toward her, lisping "heaby, heaby!"

"Yes, it is heavy," Mary laughed playfully, kneeling down, opening her arms to Jesus, and enfolding the little boy to her chest. She rocked back and forth while holding him, murmuring encouragement.

Mary looked up at Joseph from over her little boy's curls, her eyes full of gratitude. Joseph, reaching for Mary's hand, responded to the Magi, his voice cracking as he struggled to master his emotions.

"God bless you for your kindness. These gifts will prove a great blessing."

It grew late and the Magi reluctantly admitted that it was time to leave. Nike counseled with Joseph privately for a moment , then they reverently filed out of the home into the night, hoping somehow this moment could be saved in a bottle like frankincense oil. A short distance from the house they stopped and faced each other. It felt as if they had just awoken from a beautiful dream.

"Brothers," Nike exclaimed. "What — what . . . " He placed his hand in the middle of his chest, taking a deep breath and closing his eyes, as if to calm something alive inside his heart. "Who is this child? Who are his parents? We will never be the same again."

Balthazar looked up at the Star. "We will never see the same."

Nike nodded his head knowingly. "Our hearts will always be larger."

Melchior looked at his hands as if he'd seen them for the first time. "Our hands will always reach out to help."

Then Nike proclaimed: "The Child will be a great *counselor* in the tribunals of the nations. One of us must stay to observe and protect this precious instrument of the *Mighty God!*"

The other Magi, surprised at the idea of having only one person stay to protect the young king, all turned to Nike at once with the same question on their lips. "What did you and Joseph speak of before we left their home?"

Nike responded. "After our meeting with Herod I felt an urgency to take the young king and his family back to Parthia to protect and educate him, but Joseph did not want to leave Israel and felt taking Jesus and Mary to be near her family would be good for the child. We discussed our meeting with Herod and how we feared for Jesus' safety. Joseph said he would consider our offer and make a final decision in the morning."

Balthazar wondered, "do we know where Mary's family lives?" Nike shook his head surprised he'd neglected to ask.

"We will come back in the morning, we do not need to bother them anymore tonight." Nike reassured the other Magi." Secretly, he looked forward to seeing the young *prince of peace* and his mother again.

As directed, a Parthian escort arrived just outside Bethlehem, close enough for the Magi to know of their presence, but far enough away not to disturb the small town. The Magi walked slowly to meet their escort imagining if they reflected long enough, the wisps' of joy from meeting the child and his mother, might distill permanently in their hearts. But it seemed all in vain as they swung up onto their waiting mounts and rode toward camp. They could remember the intense joys of the visit with the child but they could not recreate them.

That night, the Magi's dreams were troubled, filled with God's warnings to avoid Herod and depart another way.

The Magi all awoke from their dreams simultaneously and rushed to Nike's tent to council. Nike was already up and preparing to leave for Bethlehem. A debate ensued as to whether the young king should be escorted to Rome or Parthia.

Gaspar spoke first. "The intrigue in Parthia may be just as unfit for the young king as staying here in Bethlehem!"

Melchoir queried back, "Where would you have them go? Rome has been protective of many of our royal families, but Herod is friends with Rome and the child is not safe within Herod's influence."

Nike abruptly raised his arms and interrupted. "The first order of business is at least protecting the child from Herod now. I will ride with a detachment of cavalry to secure the child and his family. We can council with them once we know they are safe."

He whisked past the other Magi, vaulting onto his Parthian stallion and galloping towards Bethlehem followed by his captain and a contingent of Parthian cavalry.

When they arrived at where the blessed family had been staying the small oil lamps were out and the cook fire was cold. Nike was beside himself. He had lost the King of Kings. He had lost him! Nike swung onto his stead and rode blindly in the general direction of the camp until his panic mellowed to a manageable despair, while he formed a plan, and his escort could catch up to him.

Nike was found staring into the sky at the star. He had regained his composer and now had a plan. He and his escort turned and cantered toward camp. Nobody dared to speak.

Nike returned to the primary bivouac where it was decided the wisest course of action would be for the other Magi and their escort to go back to Parthia by a different route.

Nike explained. "Joseph and Mary may feel we have brought too much attention to their child. Their safety was in anonymity. That is how I will find them and guard them. They will not run to Parthia and they will not flee to Rome. I must discover where they did go and beg God to give me wisdom and strength to protect them."

Nike would discover where Jesus and his family had fled and stay near enough to observe his instruction and growth but obscure as possible. He would report back to the Council as the child matured to a point where he could be invited safely into the ruling courts of Parthia. "He may be the prince of peace, The one to heal our fractured empire, and perhaps the whole world," Nike murmured.

Chapter Ten

FLIGHT FROM BETHLEHEM

Joseph reached down, gently brushing Mary's long dark hair off of her face. It tickled her nose and she rubbed it with the back of her hand without opening her eyes. Little Jesus was awake however, staring unblinking up at Joseph. Mary snuggled Jesus closer and breathed the little boy smell of sunshine and earth. Joseph hated to wake her.

"Mary . . . Mary," Joseph whispered, as he gently shook her shoulder.

"We have to leave. We have to leave now."

Mary opened her eyes and looked up at Joseph. "What a strange request," she thought.

"It's still dark outside. Why would we leave?"

"An angel visited me in a dream. Jesus is in danger, and we must flee. It seems the Magi are not the only ones who are interested in your son."

By now Mary's eyes were as wide as her little boy's as she untangled herself from the warm blanket and swung her feet to the floor. Jesus crawled off the bed and stood watching his family's movements in the dim flicker of a single oil lamp.

"How long have you been up, Joseph?" Mary asked, looking around and noticing that just a few important possessions were packed. She could see the silhouette of the loaded donkey outside the door. "Where will we go?"

"Egypt." Joseph replied. "We will go to Egypt tonight."

"Where in Egypt can we go that is safe?" Mary said, a catch in her voice. Her brow furrowed as she looked at Joseph and the anxious line of his mouth. "It is so far away . . . and the road is dangerous for our small family. We have no one to travel with!

"Do not worry, sweet Mary." He reached down and picked up Jesus, who was reaching up to him. The three embraced tightly, gaining strength from each other.

Then Joseph spoke. "The Magi's visit brought the means for our deliverance. We will find passage on a ship to Alexandria. The Jewish communities there are well established, large, and affluent. We can find work there . . . and Jesus will be safe."

Mary's face brightened and Jesus patted her cheeks and smiled touching her nose with his. The fear was broken and Joseph chuckled quietly.

Chapter Eleven

Unlikely Help

Nike spent the next few days searching for Jesus along the coast as far north as Joppa. He reasoned they might travel by ship. Nobody knew — or would say — where Joseph and Mary had taken him so he decided to go back to the Bethlehem synagogue again, desperately hoping, just maybe, he'd find just one person who knew where Jesus and his family had gone. He arrived just as the sun was rising above the horizon. He waited near the synagogue entrance under a tree.

"Sedeq!" A voice called out. Nike looked around, puzzled where the voice came from. He saw a few sheep nearby, and a donkey tied to a tree. He absently leaned closer to the donkey. Nike was not quite sure what to think. Was he hearing things now?

"Sedeq, down here!" A quiet and unusual whisper drifted up from near his feet.

Nike looked down to see a small child sitting with his back against the synagogue wall, his arms wrapped around his legs and his forehead resting on his knees. Tilting his head to the side with a wry smile, the child spoke again. "Please move. You're blocking the warmth of my morning sun."

Nike was startled. The child blended into the stone wall like he was a piece of the masonry. He slowly stepped aside, curious more than anything, allowing warmth and light to shine on the small disheveled figure.

"Thank you, Sedeq," said the peculiar voice again. "This is my favorite time of the day — the warmth of a new sun and the beautiful sounds that come with it." Nike wondered how a small child, with a voice to match, spoke with such mature language.

"Boy, look at me," he insisted, not unkindly, as he knelt next to the grey-brown figure. He wanted a better view of this interesting creature. The boy looked up slowly, and Nike nearly lost his balance. He could see the boy was blind. His face was all angles. A sharp chin, a small perfect nose, high cheekbones — and empty orbs. Like sightless white marble.

Instead of being repulsed, a breeze of compassion rustled Nike's heart. These types of feelings had increased since his visit with the young king. He could not imagine having even noticed this street urchin, let alone talk with him before. Now he felt the humanness of this child, and for some reason imagined he might help him find Jesus. No one else was.

"Why do you call me Sedeq?" Nike asked. The boy looked up again, to feel the sun on his face and to answer his question.

"You're a good man trying to do a good thing, but the path you take won't go where you expect."

Nike smiled. "You seem to know a lot about me and my journey," he replied.

This time it was the boy's turn to smile. "A wall hears many things, if it listens. Here in Bethlehem, singing skies, a child like Jesus, and Wise Men from the East make for interesting things to hear." The curious boy put his head back on his knees, then whispered audibly, like a child with a wonderful secret, "I know why you're here, and who you seek."

Nike leaned close and whispered back, "Where has the child gone? I must find him."

Raising his face to Nike's, he spoke. "He left clues about who he is. Do you want to know who he is . . . or where Joseph has taken him?"

The boy could feel Nike thinking. He paused a long time, then spoke. "I know who he is. I need to know where he went."

The boy smiled a hopeful smile. "I'll tell you where he went then, but I only ask you one kindness."

"And what is this kindness?" Nike was hesitant.

"Take me with you. I can help. I know how to find him.

Nike was quiet again while he weighed his options, then he spoke. "What is your name, extorter-of-good-men?" Nike said with a wide grin. The boy could hear kindness in his voice and he smiled back, feeling a friendship start.

"Chazon," he responded. "The last time my mother left me at this wall, she called me Chazon."

Chapter Twelve

Blind Leading the Blind

"We've spoken to, or bribed, anyone who might have seen them on the Roman road into Egypt. We've searched every port they could have left from along the Mediterranean. No one is talking, or can remember seeing the little family." Chazon, sitting against the pier, could sense Nike's fear of losing the young king. "What if Herod finds him? What if I fail at protecting him?" Nike pressed his fingers to his temples and rubbed them as if it might squeeze the answers out of his head while he complained to the air. Usually Nike had guards and attendants to do his bidding. But because of the plan to remain concealed as possible, to observe Jesus training, all he had was a curious blind boy to help him. It was overwhelming.

Chazon reached up and pulled on Nike's robes. "Sedeq, Sedeq, I have some news!" Nike was so agitated he ignored Chazon as he pulled his robe free of the boy's grasp and strode down the pier where another ship was just docking.

A few moments later, Nike returned and paced back and forth in front of Chazon.

"Gaza is the last port before heading into the desert. I can't imagine Joseph taking them into the desert or along the coast by themselves. It's too dangerous." Nike fumed. He was out of options.

Chazon tossed a piece of rope he'd found on the pier out to where he could hear Nike pacing and murmuring. Nike stopped and stared at the impetuous act.

"What?" Nike responded, not even trying to hide his irritation toward the boy.

"While you were rushing up and down these piers, I was listening. I heard some of the dock workers talking about you, and a small family running to Alexandria. I'd be happy to tell you more if you'll sit down here on the dock with me."

He patted the wooden planks next to him. "Let's put our feet in the water and I'll tell you everything I heard. Just down the pier there's a fast ship that will take us to Alexandria."

Nike meekly sat down next to Chazon. Removing his shoes, he put his feet into the warm Mediterranean.

He moved them back and forth like Chazon and felt the morning sun on his face. A calmness came over him as he remembered Jesus' love.

"I love the morning sun," Chazon said, turning his face up to the warmth. "Don't you?"

Nike looked over and watched the simple joy on the boy's face.

"I'm sorry I snapped at you," he apologized as he held the frayed rope up. "This rope figure is rather clever. You're very good with your hands . . . and your wit. I didn't realize you were making a little doll." Chazon smiled. "Before the sickness that blinded me, and stunted my little body, I drew and carved and made dolls. I can still remember everything before I went blind.

A few minutes passed and they knew it was time to go.

"Shall we get on the ship and go find Jesus?" Chazon said, as he reached out for help from Nike. Nike laced up his shoes, then pushed himself up and lifted Chazon to his feet. They walked to the ship together.

Chapter Thirteen

THE GREAT CITY

"Can you smell that Chazon? That's the smell of a great city!" Nike breathed in deeply through his nostrils and clapped his chest. Chazon stood rigid, trembling and holding onto Nike's arm.

Chazon crinkled his nose and shook his head. "There are so many different noises and so many smells. The whole world must be here. I can feel all the people. So many people . . ."

"Alexandria is a crown jewel of the Roman Empire. There are hundreds of thousands of people here, and it possesses the greatest library of knowledge ever to exist." Nike had a faraway look in his eyes, as if he'd forgotten why they were there.

"I don't know how many hundreds of thousands of people are, but if it's anything like what I'm hearing, it may as well be all the world, and we have to find Jesus amongst them all!"

This snapped Nike back into the reality of why he was there. He would have to postpone taking Chazon to the Great Library for now.

Chazon made another observation about his new surroundings, "The noises and the aromas here in Alexandria are all so different from Bethlehem. Except the fish--the fish smell the same."

Nike smiled at Chazon's joke as he formulated a plan to find Jesus. "How will we find one small family amongst so many people?" He wondered out loud. Then he turned to Chazon.

"Chazon, what do you think of this idea? Let's start by visiting the synagogues and schools in the Jewish sectors. I understand there are more Jews in Alexandria than in Jerusalem. You can sit in the markets and near the synagogues listening for clues of the little prince while I explore the Jewish quadrants of the city."

This suited Chazon just fine. He loved to listen and explore the puzzles of different people and cultures.

Nike caught himself ruffling Chazon's hair. "Can I call you Chaz?" He asked. The boy nodded and smiled a big yes as Nike pulled out a clean scarf. Then Nike continued. "I have a mission for you today. Then wrapping the scarf over his sightless eyes he explained, "Sit here against this synagogue to listen for clues of the young king. We'll disguise you as a blind beggar child with a scarf over your eyes". . .There was a long pause as Chaz and Nike realized what he had just said, then they laughed until their sides hurt.

After the laughter, Nike left Chaz with water, bread, some dried fruit and encouragement, to find clues of the fugitive family.

"I'll come back near the end of the day and collect you," he assured Chaz, who smiled, and nodded his head. Nike left him to continue his work, much like he'd found him in Bethlehem.

Chapter Fourteen

Days Become Months

Nike found Chaz where he had left him, at the confluence of the synagogue and the market. Every week they would find a new place to search for Jesus, and every week they would not find him. Not only had they not found the young king, they had not heard of any rumors of him. Hope had started to become hopeless. Chaz would always prepare an enthusiastic report to share in an effort to cheer Nike, but enthusiasm wasn't helping much anymore.

"Chaz, did you hear anything about the prince today? Any news?" Nike asked expecting another spirited story.

"I heard so many new things today Sedeq. New languages. New music. New ideas. I even heard some little children singing. But no news about the young king."

There was a long pause, then Chaz continued thoughtfully, "Back in Bethlehem I remember hearing him sing outside the synagogue about sunbeams and little streams. I've heard many songs and voices as I've listened for him here in Alexandria. But I have not heard his song. I would know his song."

Nike became distracted with an idea sparked by what Chaz was saying. "Perhaps we should move our living quarters from the middle of the more affluent parts of the Jewish community?" He mused.

All the people we know are the nobility, priests, and the affluent of the Israelites.

Chaz chimed in. "We could find a place where the Jewish district and other communities bump into each other.

Nike liked the idea and thought there was a neighborhood that matched what they were looking for towards the Great Alexandrian Library.

"You know Sedeq. I've heard rumors of excellent furniture makers and artisans near the communities against the Great Library. Perhaps Joseph could be there?"

This little revelation was the first real lead since they had arrived in Alexandria. The Jewish leaders and family connections had been unfruitful, either by choice or by ignorance, they hadn't heard of Joseph, Mary or Jesus.

Chaz piped up, "we'll do the opposite of everything we've been doing! Perhaps we'll get different results."

Nike chuckled, "yes, at least we'll get different results." He hoped.

Chapter Fifteen

A Child's Heart

The months turned to seasons and seasons to years, and still Nike and Chaz could find no trace of the young prince and his family.

Nike, sitting down and rubbing his feet, grumbled, "This was a perfect place to hide from Herod and his spies . . . and us! We've been looking for the young prince for over two years. How many Jewish businesses, schools, carpenters and synagogues are there in Alexandria?"

"Enough to keep us busy for our whole lives," Chaz chirped with a laugh. He was enjoying the adventure. "I've learned so much while listening in the markets and synagogues!"

"I know," Nike replied. "Your understanding of Greek and Egyptian is impressive."

Nike leaned down and lifted the scarf off Chaz's face and stared for a moment with a puzzled look. Chaz became uncomfortable and pulled it back down.

Nike, still baffled, pulled at his black beard and speculated. "You still look the same age as when I found you at the synagogue wall in Bethlehem. Your face is a little fuller from good food, but that's the only change from when we first met."

There was a long pause while Chaz looked down and drew in the dirt, pretending that Nike had been talking to someone else. A sand bee danced around the silence hanging between them. When the bee flew away, Chaz looked back up.

"Grownups have always let me down. They forget. They lose their curiosity and imagination. When my mother left me at the wall after my sickness, I decided to never grow up. With my blindness and small body, I imagined it was possible."

Nike kindly chided his friend. "You can't will yourself to stay young Chaz." Then, leaning back against a wall with a curious look he asked, almost to himself, "Can you?"

Chaz smiled shyly, like a child with a secret too wonderful to keep to himself. Then he spoke without turning his head, as if the small beetle walking across his foot were listening.

"Mary and Jesus would often bring me something to eat and sing to me when they came to the synagogue in Bethlehem. Sometimes Mary would sing with him, sometimes Jesus would sing by himself. They sang songs about birds and sunbeams and streams, but my favorite one was about a child's heart. Jesus sang, like he was making me a promise, that my heart would never grow old. I knew, at that moment, if I kept a child's heart I would never age or grow. This is my magic. It's magic that Jesus shared with me and I want you to have too."

Nike experienced a gentle astonishment, the type you feel when someone you think is plain smiles and you realize how beautiful they are. This feeling caused him to think back to when he was a boy. He still remembered the joy and curiosity of being a child. Nike felt a glint of jealousy for Chaz's good fortune. "How can you share your gift with me?" He teased Chaz half hoping it might be possible. Chaz replied back, not teasing. "Be patient, continue the path you follow. Have trust God guides your path, and you can achieve a child's heart."

This last proclamation left Nike distracted. For just a moment he was a boy chasing lizards and butterflies. He felt curiosity pushing out of her cocoon and the wings of imagination spreading in his chest. Putting his sandals back on, Nike made a decision. "We've been here in the learning center of the world for over two years and we haven't explored the Great Library of Alexandria yet. Let's take a holiday from looking for the young king and spend some time at the University of Alexandria."

Joseph ran his hands along the curves of a beautiful chair. "This library has wonderful furniture from all over the world," he explained as he watched Jesus explore the chair too.

"It is art and a tribute to God's love for his children." Jesus was listening intently while touching the chair with his eyes closed, moving his hands across its curves just like he'd seen Joseph do. He smiled as his small, deft fingers explored all the angles and the way the wood rolled like a scroll.

Opening his eyes, he grinned at Joseph. "Thank you for bringing me to the library, Papa."

Joseph responded enthusiastically. "We can learn from the furniture in the library and build the same type of beautiful works in Bethlehem when we go back. Perhaps we will even make pieces for the Temple itself!" Joseph seemed nearly overwhelmed with the thought.

Little Jesus was swept along in Joseph's joy and exclaimed, "For my Father's house!"

"Yes, Jesus," Joseph became a little more subdued as he remembered who Jesus Father was. "Your Father's House."

Jesus then turned from Joseph and the chair to a table nearby, surrounded by three scholarly looking men disputing a particular Greek translation of the Torah. The table was covered with scrolls. He listened to them attentively, his eyes moving from the scrolls to the faces and hands of the scholars, as they discussed the process of translating the Torah from Hebrew to Greek. The men stopped mid-discussion and looked at Jesus who was obviously listening to, and understanding, what they were talking about.

"The Greek word you are using does not mean the same thing in Hebrew. The terms may seem similar but the feeling is different." Jesus explained.

Joseph moved over to where Jesus stood watching the scholars. He ruffled his hair. "It's time to go son, your mother will be waiting for us with a wonderful meal!" Jesus reached up and took Joseph's hand, smiling and waving at the men, as he and Joseph walked out of the room. The scholars gently laughed, somewhat baffled by the bright little boy's observations.

One of the men looked back down and compared two scrolls and looked back up, his eyes like saucers, as they watched the retreating man and little boy go around a corner. "The child is correct," he exclaimed.

As they walked through the library, Joseph chatted to Jesus, explaining the different rooms and what they were for. They stopped frequently and Joseph would point out unique uses of stone and mortar. Jesus just listened and nodded his understanding.

Joseph made a proposition to Jesus. "Let's come back to the library before the Sabbath when we have more time and we can learn more about tables and listen to a lecture on the Torah's translation to Greek. We could even listen to a discussion on herbs used for healing. I understand the world's greatest library of medicine is here."

Just outside a lecture hall, a curious fly-on-the-wall listened, feeling his heart beat uncontrollably like a trapped bee bouncing in the jar of his chest. He could hear Joseph explain to Jesus the proper use of masonry and wooden beams as their voices faded down a hall.

Chapter Sixteen

Finding Him

"Hello, my friend," Nike chuckled as he reached down, grasping Chaz by his wrist to help him up from the wall.

"What's the good news?" He quipped, not expecting anything different from the last twenty four months he'd asked the same question.

"Sedeq! Joseph and Jesus were here!" Chaz laughed fervently. Before he knew what was happening, he felt his arms nearly pulled out of their sockets as Nike lifted him into the air, catching him in powerful arms.

"What did you say?" Nike cheered.

Chaz squeaked something unintelligible, and Nike realized he was squeezing Chaz so tightly he couldn't breathe.

Several library patrons walking by had startled looks on their faces as they watched a huge bearded man crushing a little blind boy in a bear hug.

Nike put Chaz down carefully and ruffled his hair, smiling a sappy grin while Chaz took gulps of air and found his balance. Two concerned women moved away quickly to avoid being the strange man's next victim.

Nike was having a hard time containing himself as he knelt down next to Chaz and, a bit more calmly, asked him to explain what he had heard again. But they were both trembling with excitement.

"Jesus and Joseph were here a few hours ago. I heard them studying and admiring a chair in the translations room around the corner! If we come back tomorrow, before the Sabbath, we may find them. I heard Joseph promise to bring Jesus back here then."

The next day, just as Chaz had promised, Joseph brought Jesus back to the library to learn more about the tables. Nike waited most of the day by the room Chaz believed Joseph and Jesus had been. "Are you sure this is the place you heard them? Chaz, who was unusually accurate about his surroundings, replied confidently, "this is the place they were. They'll be here."

Then, from down a broad corridor Chaz heard Jesus singing. His favorite song grew closer as he and Nike moved back against the dividing wall next to the room Joseph and Jesus had entered. They could hear Joseph teaching Jesus just around the corner.

"Jesus, this is the last table we can look at today. It's my favorite one. Put your hand on it, feel how smooth the surface is?" Joseph whispered in his ear. Jesus followed his example as he ran the palms of his hands across the table's surface in wide arcs.

Joseph continued, "I've watched how they smooth the surface and . . . " Then, in mid-sentence, Nike heard the sound of a slap, followed by a child's delighted giggles. He peered around the corner to see Joseph and Jesus playing. Jesus was trying to pin Joseph's hand with both his little hands on the table's surface. They were playing a game of hand-tag on the same table they had been studying. Nike had to stifle a laugh.

"We need to go home now to prepare for Sabbath," Joseph warned as he looked up through a large window, noticing how the light of the day had entered into late afternoon.

"Horsey ride?" came a question from Jesus. Joseph bent down and Jesus scrambled up his back, like a little monkey onto his shoulders. As the two entered into the crowded market outside the library Joseph rumbled his lips and neighed like a horse. Jesus giggled and buried his hands in Joseph's thick hair as they galloped away.

Like two streams converging into one roiling river, Nike felt a rush of relief and excitement all at once — They'd finally found the prince who could bring peace to the world. He had to restrain himself from running up to Joseph and Jesus to tell them how happy he was to find them as he recalled he was supposed to only observe for now.

Nike watched the two gallop away for a moment, then with a silly grin, he hoisted Chaz up on his back and they followed Joseph and Jesus while the sun rode low over the Mediterranean.

Chapter Seventeen

SURELY

Over the next two years of observing the remarkable instruction of the young king Nike taught Chaz how to write using a simple method with guides he invented. Writing expanded Chaz's already vivid and voracious mind. Chaz remembered everything with precision. Every sound. Every idea. It was like having the perfect scribe everywhere he placed him. Chaz literally absorbed all that he heard in the library, the markets and the synagogues.

"What did you learn today?" Nike asked Chaz as they sat eating dried dates on a low stone wall outside the local synagogue.

Chaz smiled and wiggled with some juicy news. "I was listening to some of the elders speaking about the new ark and mechitzah made for the synagogue."

"A what?" Nike asked with a curious grin. Chaz knew this would kindle Nike's interest.

He explained, "It seems Joseph designed and built an ark and a mechitzah for the synagogue — The mechitzah is a divider screen between the men and women for modesty. In this synagogue the men worship on the main level and the women are at the upper level behind the mechitzah. They are so happy with his work he has been asked to stand and read for the congregation."

Nike was pleased with the information and squeezed Chaz's shoulder while he looked down in thought.

"Mary may bring Jesus to hear Joseph read. I want to be there to watch and listen." Nike told Chaz.

The next day Chaz and Nike came early, disguised in common dress. They stood behind a pillar, where they could be most inconspicuous. Their plan was to listen to Joseph read and to observe Mary and Jesus. From their position behind a pillar they had a good view of all the congregation, especially Mary and Jesus.

Nike watched as the Torah was taken out of the ark and passed among the adoring assembly. Many reached out to touch or kiss the Torah scroll. When the reading of the Torah was complete another scroll, the Hephtarah or words of the prophets, was placed on the podium and rolled out to the scheduled verses for that day. It was opened to Isaiah. There was a stir of anticipation in the assembly as they heard who the prophet was. Isaiah wrote such beautiful pros about the Messiah who they all waited for.

Many swayed and rocked, covering their faces with both hands. Several women, including Mary and Jesus pressed against the beautiful lattice screen made by the man who was now reading.

Joseph hesitated as he found his place and composed himself. He recognized this scripture. Mary had read it to him on several occasions as they spoke of her son. His voice trembled slightly with emotion. Then he began:

> *Surely he hath borne our griefs,*
> *and carried our sorrows:*
> *yet we did esteem him stricken,*
> *smitten of God, and afflicted . . .*

When she heard 'Surely" Mary knew the verses he read. The words pierced her heart with joy and pain. Mary and Jesus listened intently. Jesus entwined his fingers through the screen. He looked up at his mother with awe and reverence as she bowed and rocked, quietly sobbing and pulling Jesus to her side, cradling his face. Nike watched, spellbound, as her great tears splashing down on the loft floor, launching dust into the air which swirled up on the light coming through a small window, much like his heart rose. Nike didn't know why.

*But he was wounded for our transgressions,
he was bruised for our iniquities:
the chastisement of our peace was upon him;
and with his stripes we are healed.*

Nike felt things no language he knew could describe. The same emotions that coursed through him the first time he met Jesus expanded his heart even further. He whispered to Chaz in a reverent voice, "Next to Jesus, Mary is the greatest soul I have ever encountered."

Chapter Eighteen

THE JACKAL IS GONE

It had been nearly five years since arriving in Alexandria. It seemed like only a few weeks had passed. Nike sat down near a stand of fig trees and looked out toward the Mediterranean Sea, inhaling the salt in the breeze. Pulling at his thick silvering beard, he spoke more to himself than to Chaz.

"If the rumors are true; Herod is dead. The old jackal has gone the way of all men, and all kingdoms. Israel will be in upheaval and revolution for years now."

Chaz fumbled with his dried fish and turned toward Nike's voice. His face showed alarm at this prediction. "Why revolution, Sedeq? What does this mean for the young prince?" he paused, "And us?"

Nike's mouth curved up in a sad smile as he looked back out at the storm clouds rising out of the sea.

"I've seen this before. When a tyrant dies, especially one like Herod, all his enemies will struggle for power, and to save their own lives. Rome will be drawn into the confusion to their necks. There will be revolution. Jews killing Jews. Romans killing Jews. Jews killing Romans…"

Chaz piped up naively. "Wouldn't this be a good time to approach Mary and Joseph about Jesus again?" As he said it, he could feel Nike chuckling and shaking his head. "I think we had our answer when Jesus and his family vanished that night of our dreams. We will wait for the Magi Council to signal a time when Parthia's politics are stable enough. We will approach them then."

"Anyway, it will be a few more years before Joseph can return with his family to Bethlehem. We have time for patience, and we're not looking to the young prince as a king for Judah. He is much more . . . so much more."

Chaz was incredulous that Nike or the Council didn't realize who Jesus really was yet. He prodded Nike with a question, "Who do the Magi Council think he is?"

Nike answered Chaz, "The Magi Council recognizes there is something beyond magic about the young prince. I explained that there is something of the divine about him. They suggested sending our most powerful warriors to take him back to Parthia, but I believe he is safest where he is. The council has asked me to stay close by to observe his instruction, but not to interrupt, until the time comes that we invite him to lead the Parthian Empire."

Chaz listened and reflected as he let the breeze off the sea blow his long curly hair around his face. It tickled pleasantly. "What will we do until then?"

Nike answered, "After I reported we had discovered the young prince it was decided I should be the new Parthian envoy to Rome in Alexandria. We can protect the young king here better than even in Parthia with all her political intrigues. We will observe how a young prince of the seed of David is tutored in the intellectual center of the Roman Empire."

Chaz hesitated, but decided to ask anyway. "How can I help? What can I do to protect the young king?"

Nike beamed. "You will be my personal scribe. I will use your reports to keep the Magi Council apprised of the prince's progress."

Chaz sat up straight and puffed out his chest. "Well then, I will need some new clothes befitting a scribe of the Chief Magi!" He announced.

Nike laughed so hard he tipped off his seat. He looked around to make sure no one had seen his slip and dusted himself off.

Chaz could not have been more pleased. He loved learning. He liked being with Nike. But most of all, he loved listening to Jesus learning at the synagogue's school.

Nike had been correct about the upheaval that would follow Herod's death. However, he hadn't anticipated it would require another three years for Rome to restore peace to Judah.

When Joseph heard that those who had sought the child's life in Jerusalem were dead he waited until the upheaval subsided, and Judah stabilized, before he took his family to Galilee instead of Bethlehem. Bethlehem was just too close to Jerusalem. Nike and Chaz followed.

Chapter Nineteen

BETWEEN TIME AND SHADOWS

Nike stared blankly at the parchment, only seeing his conflicting thoughts. It had been twenty years since Joseph had brought his family back to Galilee. It seemed like time had remained still for him and Chaz, as if they were in a bubble, floating on the surface of the great Euphrates River, while everything changed outside, transforming and moving as they watched.

"It's as if time doesn't matter," Nike mumbled. He rubbed his forehead, feeling very much outside himself.

He turned back to preparing his report to the Magi Council.

How long will we wait to invite Jesus to come to Parthia? You say Parthia is not ready for him. I ask if not now, when? We need him. We've spoke of a true king of kings. He is everything and more.

Nike pulled hard on his whitening beard in frustration He could literally reach out and touch the man who could unify the nations. The Magi Council was unsure, perhaps fearful like the Jewish leadership. How could he convince them? He bent down again, intent on writing a compelling paragraph to persuade the Council to bring Jesus to Parthia's courts.

> *Brothers, I've watched as the wonderful child has grown to a great man hidden in the anonymity of Galilee. Jesus's wisdom and understanding comes from something greater than the library in Alexandria or the teachings from the Jewish synagogues.*

Shaking his head in frustration he cut this section from the roll, crumpled the parchment, and threw it against the wall.

He began to scratch out his strong reasons again, dipping his quill into a brass inkwell a little too enthusiastically, spilling the ink onto the new parchment. He reached for his knife again to trim the black splatters. At this rate, he'd have to get more parchment and ink.

After wiping up the ink spill, he began to again.

> *Jesus is divine in nature. In love. In faith. And though Joseph is among the best of men, and Mary, the most noble of souls — Jesus is something more.*

Nike lifted his eyes from the parchment and stared out a window to welcome a breeze on his face and to watch how the sun and rustling leaves danced a lacey pattern on the floor. He absentmindedly licked the end of his quill without noticing he'd just dipped it in the ink pot, tattooing his tongue temporarily. He made a sour face, then bent down to write again.

If we could compress the great orb of the sun into a man, it might be enough to explain Jesus. He is the King of Kings that Parthia is looking for. He doesn't try to be kind. He is kindness. He doesn't try to love. He is love. He doesn't try to be good. He is good . . .Though he says he is not.

He is the distilled goodness of the sun in human form, living the simple yet creative life of a common man. Jesus is of the proper linage. Who better to lead the nations? Jesus is the only man capable of saving the empire. Only he can expand and keep the glory of Parthia.

He heard some commotion at the front door and quickly raised his head to see what had interrupted his important undertaking again.

"Look at this!" Chaz laughed as he dropped the corners of his tunic. Dozens of pieces of wood rattled across the floor.

Fumbling with his pen, Nike knocked the letter to the Magi Council off the table. "What in the world?" He fussed, leaning down to pick up a piece of olive wood that had skittered towards him, then paused with a confused look on his face. "How did you get here without my help? How did you get all this wood?"

A shy but pleased smile crept across Chaz face. "Jesus gave the wood to me. I was sitting, listening, and carving near where he was working. Some passers-by had just tossed a few farthings into my lap when I felt someone sit down next to me, and he ruffled my hair. I knew who it was by the kindness in his hands. He then took my hand and wrapped my fingers around a wonderful piece of sandalwood. We talked about my carvings. He gave me some pointers, but mostly he listened. Then he gave me these wood scraps and brought me home."

Nike abruptly stood up, causing the scroll he had been writing on to roll off the table again and across the floor. Sweeping past Chaz toward the door, he stumbled over assorted wood scraps as he rushed out to find Jesus. He returned moments later, unsuccessful in his search. Chaz could feel an unasked question in the air.

"He's already gone." Chaz answered. "He left me at the old date trees down by the end of our street. I knew my way from there. I could hear him walking in the opposite direction from where we'd just come, towards the wilderness. I called out and asked him where he was going. I could hear a smile in his voice when he replied, 'To spend time with my Father.'"

"It seems our covert attempts to observe Jesus have been transparent to him." Nike absently spoke to Chaz. There was a resigned relief in his voice. "Perhaps we should consider approaching him about our quest."

"Sedeq? "

Nike turned from his musings to listen to Chaz. "What if, instead of just watching him, and sending reports to the Magi Council, we try to do what he does, and help others. We could try to be like Jesus?"

Nike was stunned at the elegant simplicity of the idea. He knelt down and stared into Chaz's face, fighting the urge to lift the scarf. "What a wonderful idea! How does a small, blind, boy see so clearly?"

Chaz replied with a patient smile, "you're assuming a person has to have eyes to see."

"Close your eyes and feel this, Sedeq." Chaz placed a carved figure made of olive wood into Nike's hands. It was a game they liked to play.

"Can you guess what it is?" A broad grin brightened Nike's face as he placed it to his nose, then shook his head in satisfaction. Feeling the figure with his large fingers, he smiled again more reverently. "It's an olive wood carving of a woman riding on a donkey . . . Is it Mary and the baby Jesus?"

Chaz grinned. "Yes, it's Mary on a donkey with her baby." The fire crackled and the friends faced the flickering warmth for a long time.

"Sedeq, help me."

"Help you with what?" Nike replied, staring sleepily into the hypnotic embers.

Though still powerful and imposing, Nike was feeling his age. His beard and hair were more white than silver now, and he was vastly more patient than when he'd first arrived in Judah. He had always imagined a life of more fame, but that didn't seem as important now. He turned his attention to Chaz's question.

Chaz continued, "Up to now we've only helped a few of my friends. We can do more. We can have more friends! Our friends know others who need help. There are so many children who need someone to love them, like you love me. I want to share with them."

Nike felt something swell up from inside, just as when Jesus touched the tears on his face. Chaz always had such simple, beautiful ideas. "You're so right Chaz. Let's enlist the help of our friends to reach out to others with food and clothes."

"And my carvings," Chaz added enthusiastically.

"Yes, we cannot forget your creations. There's no room left to sit in our house." Nike pulled a piece of pine from under his leg.

Nike had just returned from visiting their new friends with dates and bread and a few of Chaz's carvings he gave out as gifts. It was good not to have so many little figures and pieces of wood all over the house.

Chaz stood by the window, feeling a cool afternoon breeze and listening to the sounds of the day.

"Chaz . . . " Nike put his hand on the boy's small shoulder. He did not respond, and seemed so deep below the waves of thought he may not have even noticed Nike's hand. He waited a moment for him to surface for air. Chaz took a deep breath, almost a sigh, and turned and smiled at Nike, tilting his head to hear what he might say. Nike was enjoying the silence too.

"Chaz." Nike finally spoke and had a hopeful note in his voice. "We've seen Jesus heal the sick, and I've heard rumors he raises the dead."

When Chaz turned back to the window and didn't say anything, he spoke again. "I've heard he gives sight to the blind."

"I've done well enough without sight." Chaz replied, almost as a challenge.

Then Chaz continued as if that small detail didn't matter. It's so nice inside here." He placed the tips of his fingers on his forehead, then gently tapped his chest. "It's a wonderful place to be. I'm not sure I want to see. It would change everything."

Nike understood a little better now. "Chaz, I think you'd like seeing the world through eyes. Imagine the adventures your wonderful mind would have with sight!"

Chaz considered Nike's argument, then observed; "would I love others more because I could see with my eyes?"

Nike had no answer and was still considering the question when Chaz interrupted his thoughts.

"Sedeq?"

"Yes, Chaz?"

"From what I hear, and from what you tell me, Jesus's greatest power is his love for his people. Isn't that the greatest power a king can have? He loves his people and they love him? His power to heal is the power of his love."

Nike was quiet for a long time. Chaz prodded him for a reply.

"Sedeq, are you still there?"

"Yes, my friend," he said with a catch in his voice. "Sometimes," he paused. "Sometimes you see more clearly than I ever will."

Chapter Twenty

It Hurts

Passover had begun, and only a few days had passed since Chaz and Nike had explored the possibility of Chaz receiving his sight from Jesus when a dispatch from the Magi Council arrived. Nike hungrily devoured every word. Then read it again, slowly, to savor the culmination of a life's work.

"Finally!" He exulted. "Finally we have been given approval to invite the Master to Parthia!" Nike left in search of Chaz to tell him the good news.

He found him at the Pool of Bethesda, one of his favorite places. It was near the Sheep Gate, at the North East part of the city. Chaz enjoyed hearing the people and animals who came through the gate and gathered near the pool. Nike found him listening to children and their mothers explaining what had just happened at the Sheep Gate.

"Chaz, great news, today is the day!" Chaz could sense involuntary tremblings of joy from Nike. "The Magi Council say it's finally time to announce our intentions to Jesus and invite him to come to Parthia!"

"Sedeq!" Chaz turned about with his hands reaching out towards Nike's voice. "You said 'we are going to visit Jesus and invite him to Parthia!' Is that what you said?" Nike nodded enthusiastically.

"Then what just happened makes even more wonderful sense!"

Nike smiled broadly and placed his hands on the boy's shoulders, giving them a squeeze. "What could be even more wonderful than taking Jesus back with us to the Parthian capital?"

Chaz, almost singing, explained, "Only a little while ago I heard an excited crowd start shouting, 'Hosanna, Hosanna, Hosanna!'" The cheering and shouting grew louder and louder and more people joined in. I could hear people cutting palm fronds and waving them in the air and putting them on the ground."

Nike interrupted, "From what I can see, there is a lot of clothing on the ground too."

"Yes," Chaz mused. "That would explain the muffled sounds from people's feet and a donkey's hooves!"

Chaz continued to tell his story, "As Jesus rode through the Sheep Gate on a donkey. The excited people all started crying the same thing, 'Hosanna to the Son of David: Blessed is he that cometh in the name of the Lord; Hosanna in the highest!' It was marvelous. It sounded as if all Jerusalem was here. Even the children were crying wonderful things! The people were laying their cloaks and palm fronds on the road in front of him. This is what people do for a king. This is what the prophets have said would happen when the Messiah would come!"

Nike wasn't sure if this was the best news he could hear. How would this affect his invitation to the Master to come to Parthia?

"This is an unexpected turn of events," Nike exclaimed. "I'm not sure how Rome, Herod, or the Parthian Empire will respond."

Nike turned to Chaz, "Whatever it means we need to find Jesus and personally deliver the invitation from Parthia." There was a long pause as the unasked question hovered in the air around them. Then Chaz spoke, "I believe it's time for me to ask the Master for my sight. I'm ready."

There were so many people around Jesus, and they were packed together so tightly, that Nike wondered if they should come back another time, but he looked down at Chaz, and the anticipation on his face, and any excuse evaporated in the day's warmth. Nike picked Chaz up with one powerful arm, and moved forward through the crowd. The people parted like the proverbial Red Sea for them until they stood next to Jesus. Nike set his friend down and waited while The King answered the complaint of a quarrelsome scribe.

It is written, My house shall be called the house of prayer; but ye have made it a den of theives. . .

As the scribe, and those with him, red faced and angry, turned and pushed their way back through the crowd. Jesus turned to the new arrivals, with a curious smile that said "I've been waiting."

"Master!" Nike pleaded experiencing a surge of the absolute love he remembered when he first met Jesus. For a multitude of new reasons grateful moisture pooled at the bottoms of his eyes. "I come with an appeal from the Magi Council and a supplication for my blind friend, Chaz."

Jesus looked up into Nike's face smiling as he squeezed his arms. He responded by gently guiding Chaz towards the Master, but instead of reaching out to heal Chaz, Jesus breathed into Nike's face as he reached up and touched his eyes.

The breath of illumination blew the scales from his eyes like dried leaves in a storm. The Master made it clear he had other plans and he expected Nike to change his.

Nike was stunned. He had been forsaken. All his passions, sacrifices and ambitions for the King meant nothing!

"Why?" Nike blurted out. "How is this possible? You are the King of Kings. How can you just throw it all away?"

Nike stumbled backward against the crowd of people surrounding Jesus pressing the palms of his hands against the sides of his forehead muttering, "What do I do now? What was it all for? All is dust. All is ashes!"

His aspirations for Jesus to be the greatest emperor the world had ever known were swept away . Instead of bringing peace and prosperity to the entire world Jesus was going to remain to teach and love this stubborn, unwashed people.

Nike looked up and stared vacantly as the great king bent down and spit into the dust, forming it with his fingers into clay that he applied to the useless orbs in Chaz' face.

"Sedeq . . . Sedeq, it hurts!" Chaz cried as he pressed the palms of his hands to his eyes. Nike steadied him. The pain and the joy Chaz was experiencing caused tears to run down his little face . . . tears experienced for the first time he could remember since he was a child. At that moment he wasn't sure if he savored the tears or the sight more.

Nike forced a defeated laugh. "Then close your eyes if it hurts. Look down. Avoid looking up for now."

"It seems," Nike murmured, "That we are both fated to leave the comfort of darkness."

"It's so exciting and confusing." Chaz sobbed as he wiped his nose with his sleeves.

"Oh Chaz, things will make sense as your mind adjusts to your new sight. You know that you're going to have to re-learn many of the things you discovered while you couldn't see. Living with sight will be different."

When they had found a place out of the sun to stand in, Chaz glanced up at Nike for a moment.

"You know, Sedeq?" He squinted still looking up. "You know, it's still fuzzy, but I like your face. You have a kind face."

"Well, Chaz, I like yours too," Nike replied as he tousled Chaz's hair and wiped his nose with the scarf Chaz had once worn to cover his blindness.

"Sedeq, I'm still having a hard time walking." Chaz put his hands out for balance, then stared in wonder at his perfect hands.

Nike reached out and took one of his hands. "Then I'll hold your hand until you can get your balance."

Chaz, hearing the defeat in Nike's voice squeezed his hand as he hugged his arm and replied, "And I'll hold your hand Sedeq, until you can know again. Let's go home."

Chapter Twenty-One

My Work Here is Finished

Nike had never felt the shock of being alone. The loneliness of abandonment. He had sacrificed everything. Didn't Jesus understand the empire, the entire world, needed him to be King! The heartbreak caused Nike to disconnect from the general news and happenings of Jerusalem. He resolved to leave this place and live out the rest of his days in anonymity.

He would go north, beyond Persia, where it was cooler and the people were fewer and kinder. Perhaps the pretentious politics that existed in Parthia or Jerusalem were not found to the north.

"Chaz, I need you to have this dispatch taken to the Magi Council." Nike handed a leather messenger wallet containing a letter with his seal.

Chaz took the letter out and turned it over in his hands, then held it up to the light as if this would enable him to see what the letter said.

"What does it say, Sedeq?"

"Chaz, you see clearly in most things . . . but you do not see well in my case. I am not a Sedeq. I am not a Saint — I am not a righteous man."

Chaz looked up shyly at Nike. "You have loved me. You've accepted me and my faith as I am. You've been my friend and encouraged me to love and help my friends on the street. They were homeless, hungry and sick. Together, we fed, healed, and clothed them."

Nike slid down against the wall to the cool stone floor. Taking a deep breath, and closing his eyes, he smiled.

"Chaz, Jesus taught me to do those things." Chaz nodded and understood better what Nike was saying.

"Sedeq. What does the letter to the Magi Council say?"

Nike, still with his eyes closed, replied, "It says my work here is done and I want to come home. It's my final report on this remarkable man who doesn't aspire to be the king of the greatest empire on earth."

Chaz seemed troubled. A mild alarm showed on his face. "Where will I go? What will I do when you go back?"

Nike laughed a deep, pleasant rumble. Opening his eyes, he wrapped his huge arm around Chaz's waist and reached up to ruffled his hair.

"Chaz! I'll take you with me, of course! You're family."

Nike noticed Chaz wouldn't look at him as he bit his lip.

"What are you so anxious about, good friend? You are coming with me!"

"Sedeq." Chaz's voice tripped in his throat. "What about . . . what about our friends who have no family?"

Nike now understood why Chaz was worried, and he replied carefully. "We will have to think about your little friends. Some still have sick bodies. We'll need to consider. . .Ah, we'll need to think." Nike was uncomfortable as Chaz stood there waiting, his hands clasped hopefully together while regarding him with a believing smile on his lips. He tried not to look back at Chaz as he handed him the message for the Magi Council. "With Passover in progress you'll need to go beyond the city gates to find a Dispatch leaving for Parthia."

Chaz took the leather wallet containing the message, and ran to where it could be sent to the Magi Council ,beyond the Euphrates, to Parthia.

Chapter Twenty-Two

IT'S TOO LATE

Nike could hear the staccato slap of sandals on the wet stone pavement getting closer. The trembling earth and unusual storm had drenched Jerusalem's streets and Nike was glad to hear Chazon running home. Since given the gift of sight, he ran everywhere. But this time, for some reason, the sound of Chaz running caused an anxious jump in Nike's chest. Something was wrong.

"Sedeq! Sedeq!" Chaz eyes were wild and frantic as he slipped around the door frame and tripped over the threshold. His knees and hands were scraped and bleeding from falling.

"What's wrong, Chaz? Nike reached to help him up. "Are you losing your sight? How many times did you fall?" Nike gently took Chaz's face in his hands and looked into his eyes, but the terror he saw was not from dimming eyesight. What he saw pierced his soul with dread.

"What are they going to do to him?" Nike cried.

Chaz, who was still out of breath, gasped, "Crucifixion!"

Nike, without waiting to hear more, abruptly turned and swept past Chaz to the cabinet that held his armor and sword.

"Chaz!" Nike roared as he threw the doors open of the cabinet that held his armor and weapons. "Help me with my armor!"

"Sedeq!" Chaz pulled on Nike's arm, trying to stop him.

Nike pulled his arm away from Chaz and yelled angrily. "If you won't help me — stay out of my way!"

Chaz stumbled back, then ran and jumped on Nike, wrapped his arms around his waist, and held on with all his might.

"It's too late," he sobbed, his heart breaking. "They crucified him!"

Chapter Twenty-Three

THE KING'S MAGIC

The room was gray and dim — but not as dim as the spirit that possessed the sobbing figure huddled in a dark corner. Since Jesus death Nike had lost the will to live, blaming himself for not being there. Chaz could not persuade him to take any nourishment, to move, or to bathe, so the scent of mildew and stale ash made the place intolerably unpleasant. Sobs of despair racked the specter, and rasping sounds emanated from his rough burlap tunic against the wall.

Nike had gone into Jerusalem in disbelief that what Chaz had told him was even possible. The general atmosphere of depression was obvious as Nike moved about city's center and the Temple. When he spoke to Roman or Jew alike they confirmed Jesus had been crucified and he was very dead. He spoke to some of those who he knew were with him and their dejection and bewilderment was something he was personally acquainted with. They were abandoned. Their lostness found it's way into Nike's soul and he was certain that he and Jesus' friends would never recover. He went home to despair.

"Sedeq," Chaz whispered as he knelt next to Nike, trying to get him to drink some water. "You haven't eaten since the master died. Please . . . " He pressed a cup of water to Nike's cracked lips. Nike turned his head away weakly.

"I asked you not to call me that," Nike's ravaged voice rasped.

"If you don't eat you'll die Sed . . . master."

Nike answered with a vacant stare and a rattling cough. Chaz jumped up and ran out of the room. "I'm going to find help!" he called out, more to himself than to Nike, as he ran to find anyone who could assist.

Nike could hear the rapid staccato of sandals on the pavement getting closer. He could tell it was Chaz coming back. A weak spark of curiosity caused him to lift his face from the stone floor for a moment.

"Sedeq! Sedeq!" Chaz eyes were wide with wonder as he slipped around the door frame and tripped over the threshold. He ran to the windows leaping to pull down the dark coverings. He threw the shutters open, letting in love-ly light and clean, fresh air.

"He's alive — He lives!" Chaz shouted as he grabbed Nike's hand and pulled to get him to sit up. Nike rolled his head, squinting at the new light, to see what was happen-ing, confused at what Chaz was laughing about.

As he began to understand what Chaz was saying, his mind started to quicken and the dry film over his eyes cleared. He started coughing uncontrollably while he propped himself up against the wall to face Chaz.

"Water!" Nike gasped. Chaz ran for a cup of water, then held it to Nike's lips. Most of the first cup ran down his filthy white beard. Chaz brought him another cup of fresh water. Nike sipped until his throat opened, then he took long, strong gulps. He struggled to get up, using the wall for support while Chaz helped him balance.

"How do you know? How do you know?" Nike kept repeating over and over, shaking his head in disbelief, until Chaz placed his hands on both sides of his face, gently holding onto his sooty beard and looking into his tearing eyes.

"I have seen His empty tomb. I heard it from his fol-lowers who saw him alive. They had no reason to lie. They had no reason to weep with joy, to pretend such elation. . .such wonder. The happiness that showed in their faces. The cries of joy in their voices. Do you remember how it felt when you met him as a child? Do you remember all the times we spoke of his love? I've only experience such light in the presence of the Master himself. He is alive."

Chaz words filled Nike, giving him strength to rise, bringing understanding of everything Jesus had revealed to him the day he opened his eyes. Throwing off the sackcloth he wore in despair, he rose to his full height and squinted against the new light; he couldn't look away, and a laugh rumbled from deep inside his chest.

"Chaz, get my best robes and armor while I wash. We have work to do!"

Nike seemed more vibrant than any young man. Hearing that Jesus was alive ignited hot embers in his heart, and an amazing transformation unfolded, starting at his core and radiating to the tips of his fingers and toes. He knew where he would go to start what he must do. The plan composed in his mind, still fuzzy but with enough clarity to move forward. Now he began to remember his purpose as the confusion, disappointment and regret began to evaporate like a fog before the sun.

"Chaz, we're leaving Jerusalem and we're taking our little friends with us."

Chaz jumped into the air, spinning like a kitten chasing a string.

"All of them?" he cried jubilantly. Nike's broad smile and enthusiastic nodding confirmed the good news. Chaz danced into the air even higher.

Nike, watching him, boomed with a laugh that had everyone in that quarter looking out their doors and windows, wondering which lunatic had had too much wine.

Then Chaz stopped in midair, landing in front of Nike with an inquisitive look on his face.

"What about the Master?" Chaz asked.

"What about Him?" Nike replied with an impetuous laugh. "He's alive and doing his work. Now we'll do what he instructed me to do when he opened our eyes. We'll bless all of the children we can, and we'll start with our homeless friends." He then explained his plans.

"We will find a place where we can be safe and grow strong. From there we will reach out to people of faith with love, and hope in their hearts."

Chaz got that inquisitive look again and asked, "What about those without faith, love, and hope?"

"Well Chaz," Nike chuckled as his friend's questions helped him remember more clearly. "Children naturally have love and faith and curiosity. Those that want to see will see us because they've chosen to be children in their hearts. To see us people will have to become like little children."

Chaz liked the answer. It caused him to vibrate with joy and almost start to float in the air. "So, where are we going, Sedeq?"

"I've heard stories of places up North, past Parthia, where empires and armies are not found. There are fewer people. We will go there with our little family. We can learn the magic of sharing as Jesus taught and then share it with the whole world."

Chapter Twenty-Four

Improbable Treasures

Nike instructed Chaz how to prepare for their adventure while he was gone learning more about what happened to Jesus. "I have some people to visit and some things to gather before we leave Jerusalem. Go and invite our friends and meet me back here, ready to leave this place."

Nike swung into his saddle and rode into Jerusalem, determined to learn as much as he could. He had to know why and how something like this could happen. Perhaps he could find something to remember Jesus with.

Nike started by seeking out the men and women who had been closest to Jesus. As they spoke of the Master , he became astonished at how blind he had been.

After learning from his friends about the events surrounding Jesus' last mortal days, he decided to start at the Temple treasury.

The priest forced a sarcastic laugh at Nike's request. "Why do you want the exact silver coins the traitor cast into the Temple? They are the price of blood. They are unclean."

"Then, what is it to you?" Nike replied back in distaste. "I will pay you well for the exact coins the traitor threw into the Temple."

Nike tossed a purse of thirty gold coins to the astonished priest, who slipped on the smooth floor as he ran to retrieve the unwanted silver coins.

"No doubt he'll find another thirty silver coins to replace the dishonored ones in exchange for thirty gold coins in his purse." Nike thought through a grim smile.

Next, as Nike rode to the Praetorium to see Pilate, he formulated a plan alongside his prayer. He realized his next treasure might be a bit harder to obtain.

"Pilate cannot see you today. He is not well." The centurion looked down to avoid looking into Nike's face.

Nike observed the assistant's behavior and mused on the fact, that with Jesus's Resurrection, it was probable Pilate was not feeling well. Nike expressed sympathy to the assistant, "I'm sorry Pilate is ill. Will you ask him a favor for me, as he knows who I am?"

"As you wish," Pilate's assistant answered evasively, avoiding eye contact with Nike. Not wanting to be drawn into the rumors of Jesus' coming back from the dead.

"Pilate's generosity is well known, and it would be appreciated if he would give me the scarlet robe used to humiliate Jesus."

The centurion looked up and stared at Nike for a moment, considering the odd request, then made a curt nod, and spun on his heel to take the appeal back to Pilate.

After a diplomatically long wait, Pilate's assistant returned, somewhat subdued from his original demeanor.

"Here is the robe you requested. It is of no use to Pilate. It is soiled."

The centurion carefully handed the bundle to Nike, who held it close to his chest, like you would hold a sleeping child. He lifted the scarlet robe to his face and inhaled as he pressed it to his cheek.

The tears streaming down Nike's face caused the centurion to soften and hesitate as he felt something —

something he remembered at the birth of his daughter — but he shrugged it off, replacing the tender feelings with embarrassment for the sentimental old Magi.

The centurion left Nike with his thoughts and went back to his administrative life. Nike turned his feet toward Golgotha, outside the city gates.

"I don't understand, my lord — why would someone like you want these rough-cut pine beams that Jesus was killed on?" The Roman commander acted incredulous. Testing what Nike was really seeking "What good will it do? It won't bring Him back."

Nike looked into the Roman commander's face and asked him a simple question, "Is that what you believe?"

With that, the commander turned to several puzzled soldiers standing nearby. "Take these beams where you are directed by this good man." The centurion walked a few paces away and returned with several large iron spikes and a circle of thorns that he reverently offered to Nike. "You might want these also."

He thanked the centurion for his kindness, then turned to viewed the city of Jerusalem and the Temple Mount. Still looking at the city, he spoke to the centurion.

"You saw what happened. Who do you say Jesus is? " The centurion walked up beside Nike and replied softly. "I believe He's the Son of God."

When Nike arrived at the place of meeting, he was greeted by happy street children. A large number of them were children he had never met. Many were malnourished and weak, but they were laughing and playing.

"Sedeq! I gathered as many friends as I could. Once the word went out we were leaving our friends invited other street children. We've been putting our caravan together just as you asked."

Nike had learned to love his new friends, but he didn't remember so many. "By what magic did you gather so many children?" Chaz just beamed back, raising his hands and shrugging his shoulders.

Nike just shook his head and gently laughed, then moved forward with his new found energy as he prepared the excited children for the adventure. "We're leaving tonight. I'll go get more supplies and animals."

Chapter Twenty-Five

As Long as Snow Falls

"Sedeq? We've brought enough supplies and animals to travel to the end of the world."

Nike laughed and looked back over at Chaz. "What makes you think we can go to the end of the world? We've only been traveling five months."

Chaz looked at the horizon where the earth met the sky. "Well, we don't eat very much. We're all so small." Nike and Chaz laughed at his joke on and off for several miles. Nike would chuckle each time he thought of the pun, and then snicker again a little while later as he remembered the sappy look on Chaz face as he said, "We don't eat very much, we're all so small."

When the laughter had subsided, Nike asked Chaz a question. "Do you want to know the place we're going?

You haven't asked the entire time we've been traveling. Come to think of it, none of our little friends have asked!"

Chaz closed his eyes and smiled, enjoying the warmth of the sun on his face. "We're together, and we trust you, Sedeq. Wherever you're taking us is a better place than we were before. And wherever we're going, we'll all be together"

There was a long quiet, interrupted only by the creaking rhythm of the horses and the gentle thud of their hooves. Chaz's face became inquisitive. "Where are we going, Sedeq?" After thinking about it Chaz had acquired some genuine interest. His tone pulled Nike out of a daydream.

"We're going to a place near the top of the world — far away from heat, politics, and pretentious people. We're going where we can be together for as long as the world stands and snow falls. We're going to where our magic can grow and where nobody can find us but we can find everyone."

Chaz's eyes and mouth opened wide. "Chaz, those eyes are a great gift. Careful, or they'll fall out." Nike laughed at his little joke and the concerned look on his face for just a fleeting moment.

"I know how you love to carve toys and figures." Nike leaned out of his saddle toward Chaz as if to tell him a secret. "Well, where we're going, there will be so many trees we'll never run out of wood for your carvings."

Chaz had a hard time imagining that many trees. "Sed-eq, if there are so many trees where we're going, why are you bringing those old pine beams under the tarp? What are they for?"

Nike closed his eyes as he worked to master his emotions. Great tears squeezed out from his eyelids, rolling down his cheeks and gently disappearing into his beard. He looked straight forward, not speaking. Chaz could tell he wasn't ready to answer that question, so he stayed quiet.

Chapter Twenty-Six

A New Home

"The mornings are getting colder." Nike mused as he looked up at the sky and smelled the wind. We've been traveling seven months north and our magic has moved us right on schedule. We're almost there, I can feel it." He then turned to his friend.

"Chaz, winter is coming and we're moving towards her. We need to start looking for a place to rest and prepare for the cold and snow. Let's look for some villages that can use our skills and will trade goods and animals with us before we reach our final destination."

Chaz looked a little concerned. "Trade what animals?" He patted the sturdy neck of his pony. The pony burped and Chaz made a sour face.

Nike chuckled that deep, happy laugh. "Have you noticed the herds of reindeer as we've come farther north?

They were made for this place. You should make friends with them."

Just then, his attention was drawn to some gray smoke floating above the trees from several villages nearby. "Take care of the family while I go arrange for a place to stay." Nike galloped off.

While Nike was gone, a small herd of reindeer wandered into camp, investigating the new people. A reindeer cow ambled over and stood nose to nose with Chaz while her new calf sucked on his fingers.

Chaz patted her neck with his free hand. "Hey girl, you're beautiful." Her huge brown eyes blinked shyly, and if a reindeer could blush, she did. While Chaz was trying to pull his fingers out of the calf's hungry mouth, she licked his face, giving him a big wet kiss.

"Looks like you've got a new admirer!" Nike said. Chaz jumped, startling the calf who bounced back behind his mother. Nike grinned.

"Sedeq! How did you get back here so quickly? Those villages are far away. It seems you only left?" Nike laughed a deep laugh that could be felt more than heard.

"Just a little magic I discovered when Jesus touched my eyes. The magic ignited when you told me that he was alive. It's the reason we are traveling so safely and quickly to our new home."

Chaz nodded thoughtfully. "I felt it when he gave me sight." He looked up at Nike and added, "Anyone who lets Him touch their eyes will find their own magic too."

The villages were larger than they'd expected, filled with happy, thriving families. They adored Nike and his little friends. The villagers gathered to welcome the newcomers. One of the clan leaders, representing most of the villages, raised his arms and asked for silence, then proclaimed, "You may stay here for the deep cold, or as long as you'd like. You bring joy to us and our children." One of the little village girls was holding a simple, but beautiful, little doll to her face, thanks to Chaz. Her smile was worth more than gold to her father, who also had wonder in his face.

Nike turned to Chaz. "Do you understand now, Chaz? Do you see how we bring joy wherever we go? The same star that guided me to the Christ Child will guide us to those who need gifts." Nike ruffled his unruly hair. Turning to the clan leaders, he thanked them for their generosity.

"We thank you for allowing us to stay in your great hall during the deep cold. Perhaps when the ice melts you can show us a good place to build our home."

This pleased the growing crowd of happy villagers, and many cheered. Especially the children holding onto wonderful little figures and toys.

Chapter Twenty-Seven

THE CARPENTER'S WORKSHOP

Nike and his little troop spent the deep cold in the great hall building big fires and telling wonderful stories. It was a happy time. Chaz and the other children had become prolific in carving and making toys, puppets, dolls, and games.

"Chaz, I don't think there are enough children in the surrounding villages for all these toys." Nike looked around in amazement. "Soon we'll have nowhere to sleep!"

Chaz jumped in the air and landed in front of Nike quivering with excitement.

"Then let's share them with all the families, in all the villages, until we run out of gifts. I've seen your magic. You move between light and shadows. It's like you live outside of time!"

Nike began laughing at this, first with a gentle chuckle, then as his joy grew, everyone in the village felt the deep vibration of his happiness. All the children in the great lodge stopped what they were doing and stared. It was a magical moment. He knew it would happen, had been waiting for it to happen, had seen it in his mind's eye. Like all magical moments, it came in its own time. . .and timing is everything in the patience of hope.

"Yes, Chaz, yes! You see so clearly! We will find the lonely, the sick, the naked, and the hungry, and take them gifts like Jesus shared His gifts. We will do it on the day the star led us to the Christ Child. Families will awake anticipating a blessing, a kindness, or a gift on this special day. This day will grow to bless the other days of the year!"

"How many toys do we have, Chaz?" Then without waiting for an answer, he continued. "Gather all those beautiful, colorful hats and warm clothes you've made. Gather all the toys, dolls, puppets, and games. Get them all ready for Christ's celebration. We have just enough time to prepare for the day of the Great King."

Then, Nike reverently went to the corner of the lodge and swept back the heavy canvas tent that covered his most valued treasures.

All the children followed him. There were the scarlet robe, the thorns, the cruel iron spikes, the thirty pieces of silver, and the pine beams: everything he'd collected before they left Jerusalem. As the children gathered around the special corner, Nike explained what each treasure meant.

Then he turned to his little band, looking into their faces. "We've work to do. Now, everyone who is not blind, will see His magic."

Chapter Twenty-Eight

CURIOSITY & IMAGINATION

During their journey north, and as winter set in, Nike had used his wisdom to teach and heal the children. Chaz taught them the art of crafting beautiful toys and warm clothes. Like Chaz, the children were happier than they'd ever imagined being. Nike was like a father to them.

As Nike was working on a particularly puzzling puzzle, he heard a soft musical sound from behind him.

"Sedeq, I don't want to grow up." Nike turned in his chair and leaned down to hear the tiny girl speak. Her voice sang like an earnest sparrow. Her huge brown eyes, on such a small face, absorbed his attention and left him unable to speak for a moment.

"What was that again, little one?" He leaned down closer to hear.

"I don't want to grow up." She repeated. Nike looked up to see Chaz smiling broadly behind her.

"I should have guessed you'd be behind this."

Chaz laughed and shrugged his shoulders. "I'm not behind anything, Sedeq. All of the children say the same thing. They don't want to grow up."

The little girl climbed up on Nike's knee and burrowed into his thick cloak. He gently patted the child's head, then looked up at Chaz.

"As long as you stay with me, and keep the curiosity and imagination of a child, you will never grow up," he promised.

The next day, Nike turned his attention to the thirty dishonored silver pieces, intent on giving them another, happier life. He bent over the coins, working carefully with fire and tools, to transform each into a clean silver bell for the reindeer harnesses. Nike labored in his magic, inscribing songs on the bells for them to sing. He held up one and waved it in the air. The alchemy of the song caused the children's hearts to flutter and everyone to pause for just a moment. They all breathed in deeply, enlivened by the beautiful music, then sprang back to work. Chaz went over to where Nike labored.

"Sedeq, was that magical music from just one bell?" Chaz asked.

Nike was surprised too. "Sometimes love and faith produce music we don't expect. These soiled coins will now become beautiful music to enter the souls of everyone who seeks the songs of healing and forgiveness. As we travel the world outside of time, people seeking to forgive, and to be forgiven, will hear the bell's songs."

Just then, four children skipped up to Nike and Chaz. They couldn't contain their excitement as they held up a beautiful red suit.

"Such perfect, small stitches!" Nike exclaimed. He examined the wonderful suit made using the scarlet robe he'd taken from Pilate. He had to kneel down so the four little tailors could help him put it on.

"Cold will never pierce this coat," he exclaimed. The joy he felt was too large to keep inside as he buried his face in the thick, rich fabric and the children hugged him.

Then, from across the room, several more children danced toward Nike with the circlet of thorns wrapped in pine boughs. They had decked it with holly and bright red berries.

"Look what we made, Sedeq. Look what we made! Can we place it on the door, Sedeq . . . can we please?" All of them jumped up and down, twirling in the air.

"I can't think of a better crown to announce which King rules here," Nike proclaimed.

"This will be a most remarkable ship!" Chaz reverently moved his hands across the sleigh's smooth surface, reaching along its scrolled wings and peering down its graceful lines. He could tell Nike was having a hard time containing his pleasure as he touched the nearly completed sleigh that had once been rough pine beams. That such instruments of pain and suffering should achieve such beauty by a carpenter's efforts of pain and love was unfathomable to Chaz. Nike gently put his carpentry tools down while Chaz continued perfecting the sleigh with his smaller tools.

"We've created something magical, haven't we Sedeq? Chaz looked to Nike knowing the answer already but asked anyway just to see the joy in Nike's face. Shall we stain it red, and polish the surface, until we can see our faces in it?" Nike smiled and nodded in agreement.

Chaz then picked up one of Nike's tools and turned it over in his hands. "Sedeq, where did you get your carpentry tools? They are well used, and they're not from around here."

Nike looked at his hands, then running his fingers along the tool's surface he looked back at Chaz. "Mary gave them to me. She didn't think Jesus would need them anymore. They had been Joseph's before that. They're a little larger than yours, but I think they will fit your hands."

Chaz face glowed, pleased Nike trusted him with something so precious.

"Continue your excellent work, Chaz. I'm going to heat the forge. Those iron spikes will stretch into superb steel runners for our sleigh."

Chapter Twenty-Nine

THE NIGHT OF THE STAR

The night of the star came quickly, but not quickly enough. Every morning the children would bounce out of their beds, run to each other and say, "Is it time yet? Is it time?"

The children and Nike had filled an immense bag, made from the tent that had covered the pine beams. Dolls, balls, toys, games, colorful hats, and warm clothes overflowed the canvas. All this was squeezed into the wonderful red sleigh, waiting for when it was time.

The Night of the Star finally arrived and Nike stood laughing next to the worthy red sleigh, the children calling to each other, "Is it time yet? Is it time?" Then Nike and the children all cried out, "Yes, it's time!" and they danced and hugged and chased each other.

As the children leaped and twirled around him, a worried look crossed Nike's face. The children noticed he wasn't laughing anymore but the twinkle in his eyes gave his mischief away, so they played along.

"Why aren't you laughing?" Dozens of concerned voices lamented as they rushed to hug Nike.

"Sedeq, please smile again. Please laugh," the children pleaded. Nike didn't expect the children's distress. He couldn't keep up the game. The children had tricked the trickster.

"I'm troubled because we have no one to pull the big red sled." All the children hopped up and down, raising their hands, begging to help pull the sleigh.

At that moment, Chaz danced into the circle waving the silver bells, fastened to beautiful leather harnesses, above his head. The music from the bells mesmerized everyone for a brief moment, then they thought they heard unusual voices just outside the circle of light.

They saw that their curious reindeer neighbors had been drawn to the happy celebration. It seemed they wanted to pull the big red sled too.

Everyone looked back and forth at each other. The children considered the reindeer and the reindeer blinked their big brown eyes and asked to pull the sled in their reindeer voices. It seemed they pleaded, "Please, we want to help too,"

Then Nike broke the stalemate.

"Children, I hope you don't mind," he chuckled, "But the reindeer want to pull the sleigh, and that's what they were made to do." Everyone cheered as Chaz and the children harnessed the excited animals.

As Nike, Chaz and a few helpers, whooshed away in the sleigh into the thick pines and swirling snow, several of the children rubbed their eyes and squinted harder. Were those wings on the reindeer swimming through the wind?

Chapter Thirty

NIKE AND THE ALFS

Nike and his helpers kept moving after they had visited all the villages around their home. They continued to spiral outward until they surrounded the whole world, leaving gifts in every place where the song of faith could be heard, or the refrain of love drew them. The giant canvas bag seemed filled with perpetual abundance. There was always a gift for anyone where Nike and the his helpers could sense hope.

Chaz glanced over at Nike, who had closed his eyes and was relishing the wind in his face.

"How is it possible that we are immune to the effects of time? Vast distances are but a walk through a pleasant garden?" Before Nike could answer, Chaz laughed with another question", and why do our gifts keep multiplying . . . We should have given them all away long ago."

Nike wasn't fully sure how to answer Chaz's questions, he didn't know yet how to explain the physics of what he knew. The explanation floated there waiting to be born. This was a first for him too. He turned his face forward again where the wind uncovered a peace in his face, as if he were praying.

After Chaz's anticipation for an answer had dozed off, Nike turned back to his inquisitive friend. "I have an idea. Even a suspicion that the illusion of limit is like the twinkle of a star, it is only perceived."

Nike then raised his voice above the wind and explained the magic of the canvas bag to Chaz. "Do you remember the story we heard of the miracle of the loaves and fishes. I think the canvas bag is similar. Its power comes from the miracle of people whose hearts, like the bag, are full of abundance. Hope and Love are not limited by space, or distance, or any time piece."

Chaz was delighted by Nike's answer, it meant there would always be more magic to discover. He turned his face into the wind and inhaled a breath of kindness, then scrambled back and looked into the nearly empty canvas bag.

"Sedeq, it looks like we have one more stop to make before we go home."

Nike brought the sled down near a remote cottage where a widow and her two hungry children lived. They quietly delivered their final gifts, being careful not to wake the children. They hid outside the cottage window and listened while the family awoke to a crackling fire, food stacked against the walls, and warm new clothes. The two little girls each found a lovely doll in their new wool stockings. The youngest little girl turned to her mother, whose emotions had overwhelmed her voice. "Mama, remember the stories you told us about the Alf-Heim? Did they bring us these gifts?" The mother nodded her head, her voice still captive to joy.

"Alf have been here, mother! The Alf have been here and helped us when things were darkest!" The mother responded by falling to her knees and pulling her two little girls tightly to her chest as she sobbed something about the wonderful Alf.

The helpers, who had moved the sleigh into the forest, crept up to see what Nike and Chaz were doing near the small frosted window. What they all saw caused them to grin with glee and laugh quietly, blowing out breaths full of frosty stars.

Chaz had a beautiful, curious look on his face when he asked, "The people here call us Alfs. What's an Alf?"

Nike leaned back and chuckled. "They call you earthbound angels."

Chaz face brightened. "Then, from now on, we'll be called Alfs! Nike and his Alfs!"

Chapter Thirty-One

A CHOICE OF FAITH

Bix looked up from reading the story. He had no doubts about Santa Clause, and more important-ly who Christmas was all about. He looked up at the people who loved him most and he saw in their eyes what he felt in his heart. They may have been the only family he had left, but they were more than enough.

Newt fervently whispered, "I knew it! I just new it. Dad was right, there is a Saint Nicholas."

Agnes and Mom smiled quietly, still amazed by the story. No one even thought to look at a watch or phone as they enjoyed the warmth that enveloped them. They were lost in thoughts of each other and Newt Sr. and the gifts he had given them.

Bix broke the silence. "Newt, thank you for sharing this story and your faith." Agnes nodded in agreement. Erin just leaned back into the couch with her eyes closed, clasping a pillow to her chest. A tear finding its way down her cheek.

Newt's story about the Magi, and finally knowing what had happened to him, propelled the family above the inversion of gloom that had oppressed them for three years. They were able to breath and laughed and visit about things that had depressed them only a few hours before. They were able to look to a brighter future, as they waited with Newt Jr. every Christmas Eve at the front door for Santa. Christmas was now an exercise of patience and hope. They would see Newt again. They would celebrate this joy every year as they read about the Magi's Christmas.

Bix looked at his watch realizing Christmas Eve had become Christmas morning. Really early Christmas morning. "It's late, I mean early, I mean I should go Thank you for this wonderful Christmas Eve!"

As Bix got up to leave, Newt jumped up and hugged him, pinning his arms to his side. Agnes and Erin followed and a group hug ensued.

"Our home is your home, Bix. Never forget that," Erin whispered. Everyone squeezed a little harder.

"Will Uncle Bix come back over for Christmas tomorrow, I mean today?" Newt blurted. From the look on everyone's faces, it was a question that didn't need to be asked.

"I'll come back," Bix laughed. "I just need to pick a few things up at home and clean up a bit!"

Chapter Thirty-Two

ONE YEAR TO THE DAY

The drapes were open, and it was a clear, cold Christmas Eve. The moon was so bright, it hurt to look at it. Even the stealthiest mouse might be seen on this night. A shadow moved almost imperceptibly across the living room floor toward the Christmas tree.

"Bix," a whisper came from a dark corner where the moonlight didn't reach. Bix almost dropped the package he carried as an involuntary squeak escaped his throat. A soft laugh came from the dark.

"Bix, come over here and sit down."

Bix carefully moved toward the voice where Erin sat curled up under a quilt. "Please sit down, Bix." She patted the cushion next to her. He tentatively sat next to Erin.

"How did you know I was coming back tonight?" Bix protested. Erin gently pressed her fingers to his lips.

"Lower your voice, and listen." Then, looking into his eyes, she tenderly spoke.

"I knew you were coming because you've always been there for my family. You were always there for Newt. You pulled him out of some tight spots. You've been there for Newt Jr. when he needed a strong man to talk with, and for Agnes when she needed someone to listen, someone who loved her other than her mother.

My children need a good man in their life. Since their father died, there is an ache that echoes in our lives too frequently. It's been a year since we discovered what happened to Newt. You've stepped in and helped so many times since he went missing. You've been such a great part of this family . . . You've been a good friend to me."

Bix looked down quickly. He wasn't sure what was happening. Was Erin proposing to him? He looked back up to make sure. Yes, she was in earnest.

"Bix." Erin leaned over and brushed his cheek with her lips while she squeezed his hand. "We can talk more about this when you come over in the morning for Christmas with the family."

Bix, a little dazed, got up and stumbled toward the door, still clutching the package he'd come to deliver.

"Oh Bix," Erin giggled with a smile. "Leave the gift. I'll put it under the tree."

Christmas morning, the family gathered for Mom's special Christmas breakfast. It was good to have Uncle Bix there with them.

"How do you like those monkey bites, Bix?" Agnes teased. Bix popped a piece into his mouth and washed it down with milk.

"Why do you think I came for Christmas breakfast?" He laughed, looking over at Erin with a bashful grin.

Agnes rescued the last delicious morsel off Bix's plate while he was trying to spear another bite off Newt's.

"Thanks for being here for Christmas, Bix." Erin said. Agnes and Newt nodded their agreement, their mouths still stuffed with food.

After breakfast, Agnes put on some Christmas tunes and everyone gathered around the tree to talk and share gifts. When most of the presents had been shared, Newt noticed something shiny on the tree's lower branches.

"What's this?" Newt stooped down and lifted a silver bell off a tree branch. He sat on the floor and held it up to the light.

"That's beautiful, Newt!"

Agnes crawled through some wrapping paper to get a closer look.

"It's so delicate; It looks like a real silver bell . . . like you see on horse harnesses," Agnes said with awe.

"Or a reindeer harness," Newt grinned.

Agnes gently grasped Newt's hand and shook it back and forth. The pure sounds from the bell were clean and crisp, a song of promise. The bell had four delicate leaves curved down with intricate scrolling. A delicate script circled the bell in a language they hadn't seen before. Everyone looked at Erin.

"Mom, where did you get this silver bell?" Agnes turned to face her mother, still holding onto Newt's hand and the silver bell.

"I've never seen it before. It is so exquisite!" Now Erin crawled through the wrapping paper to get a better look.

Newt handed the hypnotizing bauble to his mother. Everyone then turned and looked at Bix. They were rewarded with a silly smile and a shrug of his shoulders.

Bix began the wrapping paper pilgrimage, wincing as he knelt on a hard candy.

"I've never seen anything like this." Then he shook it again, reverently, and everyone closed their eyes and sighed with the most peaceful smile on their faces. They were silent for a few moments, cherishing the beautiful sound.

Agnes whispered, "It's one of the bells from the reindeer harnesses."

Without responding, Bix reached under the tree and pulled out a package wrapped in simple brown paper. It was the same gift he'd tried to sneak under the tree earlier that morning. He handed it to Newt.

"They found the manuscript your father was translating in the belongings of an enemy commander they captured. They were able to identify it by letters from your family between some of the pages. After confirming there were no top secret materials, Intelligence contacted me and asked if you wanted it."

Newt carefully unwrapped the ancient text. It smelled of an interesting combination of oil, mildew, and smoke. Centuries of wear and repair stained the leather cover.

"Dad must have been carrying it when he disappeared during the firefight," Newt held the manuscript up, nearly touching it to his mouth and nose. He inhaled the musky tang of the book and opened the uneven, mismatched pages. Some gray-brown dust drifted into the sunlight and danced with the other dust motes.

The pages differed in material and writing, but left the same magical feeling with each new leaf turned.

"This is so great!" Newt spoke with an enthusiastic whisper, then handed the leather text to his mother. The family spent the rest of the afternoon holding the book, turning the pages, and sharing stories about their dad and brother. This had been a perfect Christmas.

The next morning Mom and Agnes woke late. Newt had been up for a while doing Newtish things and poking around the house. It seemed like Christmas had been a dream, and he wanted to find evidence it had all happened. He called out to himself and anyone who would listen.

"Has anyone seen the silver bell? It was right here on the Magi's Christmas story."

Newt wanted to look at the book and listen to the music of the bell again. But it wasn't on the mantle, where he had carefully left it the night before.

He called to his mother. "Mom, do you know where the bell is?"

"I haven't seen it. I'll call your uncle and see what he knows," she called back from the kitchen.

Agnes walked into the room with her mouth full of leftover turkey. "It wasn't there this morning?"

Erin came in after calling Uncle Bix to ask him if he'd barrowed the bell when he left late after visiting with her. He hadn't.

"He saw it on the mantle with the book when he went home," said Erin with a note of concern in her voice.

Instead of getting upset, Newt became more excited.

"I suppose we can only have it for one day a year. " Newt grinned. "That's good enough for me."

Outside of time, between light and shadows, Chaz shook the beautiful silver sleigh bell gently near his ear.

"I hope you're happy with yourself," Saint Nike scolded kindly. "With the kind of faith that boy has, we're going to have to do this every year."

Chaz, still holding the bell to his ear replied, "oh, I didn't tell you? There are a few more missing bells we need to retrieve!" And he laughed and laughed.

ABOUT THE AUTHOR

Noel is a serial entrepreneur and writer that Don Quixote would be proud of. He's the author of: Magi's Christmas...33 Years to Easter.

For two decades he's been irritated by the uninspiring, two dimensional, portrayal of the Wisemen's visit to the child Jesus. That irritation, like a grain of sand in an oyster, has birthed a pearl of historical fiction, reflecting the truth of the Magi and a renewal of Christmas Joy.

Noel writes from a tall, white farmhouse, on the porch, in the middle of 20 acres with a spectacular view of the western approach to the Rocky Mountains.

GRAIN OF SAND

When I was 11 years old the local newspaper held a Christmas card contest. My entry was a black ink silhouette of the three Wise Men riding camels across the desert. Mom proudly taped the picture to the refrigerator.

At the time, I didn't think much about it. Most folks still believe three Magi crossed a vast wilderness to bring gold, frankincense, and myrrh to the baby Jesus. How would I know any different? I was a kid delivering newspapers in a mining town. But then, an idea, like a grain of sand, imbedded itself in my imagination, the way sand does in an oyster to create a pearl.

From that time forward, every Christmas card with a star or the Magi on it caused me to ask: Why in the world would three "Wise Men", called kings, traverse the breadth of a dangerous wilderness to leave expensive gifts for Jesus, then go back to their kingdoms? It didn't make sense. I started asking questions and researching who the Wise Men were and where they came from. What I found was fascinating.

I learned the Magi saw the star at Christ's birth, but that they didn't arrive to worship the child until nearly two years later.

I also found that the Magi were most likely from the Parthian Empire which had replaced the Persian Empire. Rome and Parthia had been at war and were at an uneasy truce at the time of Jesus' birth.

The Parthian Empire was at least Rome's equal if not its superior. Rome had tried to conquer Parthia, and were soundly defeated on several occasions, deeply humiliating Rome, and costing them tens of thousands of their best troops.

The Magi were Parthia's Kingmakers. They chose Parthia's kings and impeached unfit rulers. The Magi were power brokers and it was not by accident they made an epic journey to worship the child Jesus. The very heavens had declared the child was the King of Kings.

So, here was this little boy, Mary's son, at the nexus of the two greatest empires in the world and one of those empires was sending the Magi, who chose Parthia's kings, right to his front door.

This is an epic story, historically authentic, with the alchemy of fantasy woven into it. It is a story-journey we must all go through. It addresses the joys of family and the singular experience of being alone.

From meager souls to the mighty and powerful, everyone must eventually make their journey through Christmas. Everyone.

Made in the USA
San Bernardino, CA
23 November 2018